François Coppée, And others

Stories by Foreign Authors

French

François Coppée, And others

Stories by Foreign Authors
French

ISBN/EAN: 9783337279462

Printed in Europe, USA, Canada, Australia, Japan

Cover: Foto ©Andreas Hilbeck / pixelio.de

More available books at **www.hansebooks.com**

STORIES BY
FOREIGN AUTHORS

FRENCH

NEW YORK
CHARLES SCRIBNER'S SONS
1901

PUBLISHERS' NOTE

The translations in this volume, where previously published, are used by arrangement with the owners of the copyrights (as specified at the beginning of each story). Translations made especially for the series are covered by its general copyright. All rights in both classes are reserved.

CONTENTS

THE SUBSTITUTE

BY

FRANCOIS COPPÉE

From " Ten Tales by François Coppée." Translated by
Walter Learned. Published by Harper & Bros.

THE SUBSTITUTE

BY FRANCOIS COPPÉE

HE was scarcely ten years old when he was first arrested as a vagabond.

He spoke thus to the judge:

"I am called Jean François Leturc, and for six months I was with the man who sings and plays upon a cord of catgut between the lanterns at the Place de la Bastille. I sang the refrain with him, and after that I called, 'Here's all the new songs, ten centimes, two sous!' He was always drunk, and used to beat me. That is why the police picked me up the other night. Before that I was with the man who sells brushes. My mother was a laundress, her name was Adèle. At one time she lived with a man on the ground-floor at Montmartre. She was a good work-woman and liked me. She made money because she had for customers waiters in the cafés, and they use a good deal of linen. On Sundays she used to put me to bed early so that she could go to the ball. On week-days she sent me to Les Frères, where I learned to read.

Well, the sergent-de-ville whose beat was in our street used always to stop before our windows to talk with her—a good-looking chap, with a medal from the Crimea. They were married, and after that everything went wrong. He did n't take to me, and turned mother against me. Every one had a blow for me, and so, to get out of the house, I spent whole days in the Place Clichy, where I knew the mountebanks. My father-in-law lost his place, and my mother her work. She used to go out washing to take care of him; this gave her a cough—the steam. . . . She is dead at Lamboisière. She was a good woman. Since that I have lived with the seller of brushes and the catgut scraper. Are you going to send me to prison?"

He said this openly, cynically, like a man. He was a little ragged street-arab, as tall as a boot, his forehead hidden under a queer mop of yellow hair.

Nobody claimed him, and they sent him to the Reform School.

Not very intelligent, idle, clumsy with his hands, the only trade he could learn there was not a good one—that of reseating straw chairs. However, he was obedient, naturally quiet and silent, and he did not seem to be profoundly corrupted by that school of vice. But when, in his seventeenth year, he was thrown out again on the streets of Paris, he unhappily found there his pris-

on comrades, all great scamps, exercising their
dirty professions : teaching dogs to catch rats in
the sewers, and blacking shoes on ball nights in
the passage of the Opera—amateur wrestlers, who
permitted themselves to be thrown by the Her-
cules of the booths—or fishing at noontime from
rafts ; all of these occupations he followed to
some extent, and, some months after he came out
of the house of correction, he was arrested again
for a petty theft—a pair of old shoes prigged
from a shop-window. Result : a year in the prison of Sainte Pélagie, where he served as valet
to the political prisoners.

He lived in much surprise among this group
of prisoners, all very young, negligent in dress,
who talked in loud voices, and carried their heads
in a very solemn fashion. They used to meet in
the cell of one of the oldest of them, a fellow of
some thirty years, already a long time in prison
and quite a fixture at Sainte Pélagie—a large
cell, the walls covered with colored caricatures,
and from the window of which one could see all
Paris—its roofs, its spires, and its domes—and
far away the distant line of hills, blue and indis-
tinct upon the sky. There were upon the walls
some shelves filled with volumes and all the old
paraphernalia of a fencing-room : broken masks,
rusty foils, breastplates, and gloves that were
losing their tow. It was there that the " poli-
ticians " used to dine together, adding to the

everlasting "soup and beef," fruit, cheese, and pints of wine which Jean François went out and got by the can—a tumultuous repast interrupted by violent disputes, and where, during the dessert, the "Carmagnole" and "Ça Ira" were sung in full chorus. They assumed, however, an air of great dignity on those days when a new-comer was brought in among them, at first entertaining him gravely as a citizen, but on the morrow using him with affectionate familiarity and calling him by his nickname. Great words were used there: Corporation, Responsibility, and phrases quite unintelligible to Jean François—such as this, for example, which he once heard imperiously put forth by a frightful little hunch-back who blotted some writing-paper every night:

"It is done. This is the composition of the Cabinet: Raymond, the Bureau of Public Instruction; Martial, the Interior; and for Foreign Affairs, myself."

His time done, he wandered again around Paris, watched afar by the police, after the fashion of cockchafers, made by cruel children to fly at the end of a string. He became one of those fugitive and timid beings whom the law, with a sort of coquetry, arrests and releases by turn—something like those platonic fishers who, in order that they may not exhaust their fish-pond, throw immediately back into the water the fish which has just come out of the net. Without a suspicion

on his part that so much honor had been done to
so sorry a subject, he had a special bundle of
memoranda in the mysterious portfolios of the
Rue de Jérusalem. His name was written in
round hand on the gray paper of the cover, and
the notes and reports, carefully classified, gave
him his successive appellations: "Name, Leturc;" "the prisoner Leturc," and, at last, "the
criminal Leturc."

He was two years out of prison, dining where
he could, sleeping in night lodging-houses and
sometimes in lime-kilns, and taking part with his
fellows in interminable games of pitch-penny on
the boulevards near the barriers. He wore a
greasy cap on the back of his head, carpet slip-
pers, and a short white blouse. When he had
five sous he had his hair curled. He danced at
Constant's at Montparnasse; bought for two
sous to sell for four at the door of Bobino, the
jack of hearts or the ace of clubs serving as a
countermark; sometimes opened the door of a
carriage; led horses to the horse-market. From
the lottery of all sorts of miserable employments
he drew a goodly number. Who can say if the
atmosphere of honor which one breathes as a
soldier, if military discipline might not have
saved him? Taken, in a cast of the net, with
some young loafers who robbed drunkards sleeping on the streets, he denied very earnestly having taken part in their expeditions. Perhaps he

2

told the truth, but his antecedents were accepted
in lieu of proof, and he was sent for three years
to Poissy.   There he made coarse playthings for
children, was tattooed on the chest, learned
thieves' slang and the penal code.   A new libera-
tion, and a new plunge into the sink of Paris;
but very short this time, for at the end of six
months at the most he was again compromised
in a night robbery, aggravated by climbing and
breaking—a serious affair, in which he played an
obscure rôle, half dupe and half fence.   On the
whole his complicity was evident, and he was
sent for five years at hard labor.   His grief in
this adventure was above all in being separated
from an old dog which he had found on a dung-
heap, and cured of the mange.   The beast loved
him.

Toulon, the ball and chain, the work in the
harbor, the blows from a stick, wooden shoes on
bare feet, soup of black beans dating from
Trafalgar, no tobacco money, and the terrible
sleep in a camp swarming with convicts; that
was what he experienced for five broiling sum-
mers and five winters raw with the Mediterranean
wind.   He came out from there stunned, was
sent under surveillance to Vernon, where he
worked some time on the river.   Then, an incorrigible vagabond, he broke his exile and came
again to Paris.   He had his savings, fifty-six
francs, that is to say, time enough for reflection.

During his absence his former wretched companions had dispersed. He was well hidden, and
slept in a loft at an old woman's, to whom he represented himself as a sailor, tired of the sea,
who had lost his papers in a recent shipwreck,
and who wanted to try his hand at something
else. His tanned face and his calloused hands,
together with some sea phrases which he dropped
from time to time, made his tale seem probable
enough.

One day when he risked a saunter in the
streets, and when chance had led him as far as
Montmartre, where he was born, an unexpected
memory stopped him before the door of Les
Frères, where he had learned to read. As it was
very warm the door was open, and by a single
glance the passing outcast was able to recog-
nize the peaceable school-room. Nothing was
changed : neither the bright light shining in at the
great windows, nor the crucifix over the desk, nor
the rows of benches with the tables furnished
with inkstands and pencils, nor the table of
weights and measures, nor the map where pins
stuck in still indicated the operations of some
ancient war. Heedlessly and without thinking,
Jean François read on the blackboard the words of
the Evangelist which had been set there as a copy :

" Joy shall be in heaven over one sinner that
repenteth, more than over ninety and nine just
persons, which need no repentance."

It was undoubtedly the hour for recreation, for
the Brother Professor had left his chair, and, sitting on the edge of a table, he was telling a story
to the boys who surrounded him with eager and
attentive eyes.   What a bright and innocent face
he had, that beardless young man, in his long
black gown, and white necktie, and great ugly
shoes, and his badly cut brown hair streaming
out behind !   All the simple figures of the children of the people who were watching him seemed
scarcely less childlike than his ; above all when,
delighted with some of his own simple and priestly
pleasantries, he broke out in an open and frank
peal of laughter which showed his white and regular teeth, a peal so contagious that all the scholars
laughed loudly in their turn.   It was such a sweet,
simple group in the bright sunlight, which lighted
their dear eyes and their blond curls.

Jean François looked at them for some time in
silence, and for the first time in that savage
nature, all instinct and appetite, there awoke a
mysterious, a tender emotion.   His heart, that
seared and hardened heart, unmoved when the
convict's cudgel or the heavy whip of the watch-
man fell on his shoulders, beat oppressively.   In
that sight he saw again his infancy ; and closing
his eyes sadly, the prey to torturing regret, he
walked quickly away.

Then the words written on the blackboard
came back to his mind.

"If it was n't too late, after all!" he murmured; "if I could again, like others, eat
honestly my brown bread, and sleep my fill without nightmare! The spy must be sharp who
recognizes me. My beard, which I shaved off
down there, has grown out thick and strong.
One can burrow somewhere in the great ant-hill,
and work can be found. Whoever is not worked
to death in the hell of the galleys comes out agile
and robust, and I learned there to climb ropes
with loads upon my back. Building is going on
everywhere here, and the masons need helpers.
Three francs a day! I never earned so much.
Let me be forgotten, and that is all I ask."

He followed his courageous resolution; he
was faithful to it, and after three months he was
another man. The master for whom he worked
called him his best workman. After a long day
upon the scaffolding, in the hot sun and the dust,
constantly bending and raising his back to take
the hod from the man at his feet and pass it to
the man over his head, he went for his soup to
the cook-shop, tired out, his legs aching, his
hands burning, his eyelids stuck with plaster, but
content with himself, and carrying his well-earned
money in a knot in his handkerchief. He went
out now without fear, since he could not be recognized in his white mask, and since he had
noticed that the suspicious glances of the police-
man were seldom turned on the tired workman.

He was quiet and sober. He slept the sound
sleep of fatigue. He was free !

At last—oh, supreme recompense !—he had
a friend !

He was a fellow-workman like himself,
named Savinien, a little peasant with red lips
who had come to Paris with his stick over his
shoulder and a bundle on the end of it, fleeing
from the wine-shops and going to mass every
Sunday. Jean François loved him for his piety,
for his candor, for his honesty, for all that he
himself had lost, and so long ago. It was a passion, profound and unrestrained, which trans-
formed him by fatherly cares and attentions.
Savinien, himself of a weak and egotistical nature,
let things take their course, satisfied only in
finding a companion who shared his horror of the
wine-shop. The two friends lived together in a
fairly comfortable lodging, but their resources
were very limited. They were obliged to take
into their room a third companion, an old Auvergnat, gloomy and rapacious, who found it possible out of his meagre salary to save something
with which to buy a place in his own country.
Jean François and Savinien were always together.
On holidays they together took long walks in the
environs of Paris, and dined under an arbor in
one of those small country inns where there are a
great many mushrooms in the sauces and innocent rebusses on the napkins. There Jean Fran-

çois learned from his friend all that lore of which
they who are born in the city are ignorant;
learned the names of the trees, the flowers, and
the plants; the various seasons for harvesting;
he heard eagerly the thousand details of a labo-
rious country life—the autumn sowing, the winter
chores, the splendid celebrations of harvest and
vintage days, the sound of the mills at the water-
side, and the flails striking the ground, the tired
horses led to water, and the hunting in the morning mist; and, above all, the long evenings around
the fire of vine-shoots, that were shortened by
some marvellous stories. He discovered in
himself a source of imagination before unknown,
and found a singular delight in the recital of
events so placid, so calm, so monotonous.

One thing troubled him, however: it was the
fear lest Savinien might learn something of his
past. Sometimes there escaped from him some
low word of thieves' slang, a vulgar gesture—
vestiges of his former horrible existence—and he
felt the pain one feels when old wounds re-open;
the more because he fancied that he sometimes
saw in Savinien the awakening of an unhealthy
curiosity. When the young man, already tempted
by the pleasures which Paris offers to the poorest, asked him about the mysteries of the great
city, Jean François feigned ignorance and turned
the subject; but he felt a vague inquietude for
the future of his friend.

His uneasiness was not without foundation. Savinien could not long remain the simple rustic that he was on his arrival in Paris. If the gross and noisy pleasures of the wine-shop always repelled him, he was profoundly troubled by other temptations, full of danger for the inexperience of his twenty years. When spring came he began to go off alone, and at first he wandered about the brilliant entrance of some dancing-hall, watching the young girls who went in with their arms around each other's waists, talking in low tones. Then, one evening, when lilacs perfumed the air and the call to quadrilles was most captivating, he crossed the threshold, and from that time Jean François observed a change, little by little, in his manners and his visage. He became more frivolous, more extravagant. He often borrowed from his friend his scanty savings, and he forgot to repay. Jean François, feeling that he was abandoned, jealous and forgiving at the same time, suffered and was silent. He felt that he had no right to reproach him, but with the foresight of affection he indulged in cruel and inevitable presentiments.

One evening, as he was mounting the stairs to his room, absorbed in his thoughts, he heard, as he was about to enter, the sound of angry voices, and he recognized that of the old Auvergnat who lodged with Savinien and himself. An old habit of suspicion made him stop at the landing-place and listen to learn the cause of the trouble.

"Yes," said the Auvergnat, angrily, "I am sure that some one has opened my trunk and stolen from it the three louis that I had hidden in a little box; and he who has done this thing must be one of the two companions who sleep here, if it were not the servant Maria. It concerns you as much as it does me, since you are the master of the house, and I will drag you to the courts if you do not let me at once break open the valises of the two masons. My poor gold! It was here yesterday in its place, and I will tell you just what it was, so that if we find it again nobody can accuse me of having lied. Ah, I know them, my three beautiful gold-pieces, and I can see them as plainly as I see you! One piece was more worn than the others; it was of greenish gold, with a portrait of the great emperor. The other was a great old fellow with a queue and epaulettes; and the third, which had on it a Philippe with whiskers, I had marked with my teeth. They don't trick me. Do you know that I only wanted two more like that to pay for my vineyard? Come, search these fellows' things with me, or I will call the police! Hurry up!"

"All right," said the voice of the landlord; "we will go and search with Maria. So much the worse for you if we find nothing, and the masons get angry. You have forced me to it."

Jean François' soul was full of fright. He re-membered the embarrassed circumstances and the small loans of Savinien, and how sober he had seemed for some days. And yet he could not believe that he was a thief. He heard the Auvergnat panting in his eager search, and he pressed his closed fists against his breast as if to still the furious beating of his heart.

"Here they are!" suddenly shouted the victorious miser. "Here they are, my louis, my dear treasure; and in the Sunday vest of that little hypocrite of Limousin! Look, landlord, they are just as I told you. Here is the Napo-leon, the man with a queue, and the Philippe that I have bitten. See the dents! Ah, the little beggar with the sanctified air. I should have much sooner suspected the other. Ah, the wretch! Well, he must go to the convict prison."

At this moment Jean François heard the well-known step of Savinien coming slowly up the stairs.

He is going to his destruction, thought he. Three stories. I have time!

And, pushing open the door, he entered the room, pale as death, where he saw the landlord and the servant stupefied in a corner, while the Auvergnat, on his knees, in the disordered heap of clothes, was kissing the pieces of gold.

"Enough of this," he said, in a thick voice; "I took the money, and put it in my comrade's trunk. But that is too bad. I am a thief, but not a Judas. Call the police; I will not try to escape, only I must say a word to Savinien in private. "Here he is."

In fact the little Limousin had just arrived, and seeing his crime discovered, believing himself lost, he stood there, his eyes fixed, his arms hanging.

Jean François seized him forcibly by the neck, as if to embrace him; he put his mouth close to Savinien's ear, and said to him in a low, supplicating voice:

"Keep quiet."

Then turning towards the others:

"Leave me alone with him. I tell you I won't go away. Lock us in if you wish, but leave us alone."

With a commanding gesture he showed them the door.

They went out.

Savinien, broken by grief, was sitting on the bed, and lowered his eyes without understanding anything.

"Listen," said Jean François, who came and took him by the hands. "I understand! You have stolen three gold-pieces to buy some trifle for a girl. That costs six months in prison. But one only comes out from there to go back again, and you will become a pillar of police courts and tribunals. I understand it. I have been seven years at the Reform School, a year at Sainte Pélagie, three years at Poissy, five years at Toulon. Now, don't be afraid. Everything is arranged. I have taken it on my shoulders."

"It is dreadful," said Savinien; but hope was springing up again in his cowardly heart.

"When the elder brother is under the flag, the younger one does not go," replied Jean François. "I am your substitute, that's all. You care for me a little, do you not? I am paid. Don't be childish—don't refuse. They would have taken me again one of these days, for I am a runaway from exile. And then, do you see, that life will be less hard for me than for you. I know it all, and I shall not complain if I have not done you this service for nothing, and if you swear to me that you will never do it again. Savinien, I have loved you well, and your friendship has made me happy. It is through it that, since I have known you, I have been honest and pure, as I might always have been, perhaps, if I had had, like you, a father to put a tool in my hands, a mother to teach me my prayers. It was my sole regret that I was useless to you, and that I deceived you concerning myself. To-day I have unmasked in saving you. It is all right. Do not cry, and embrace me, for already I hear heavy boots on the stairs. They are coming with the *posse*, and we must not seem to know each other so well before those chaps."

He pressed Savinien quickly to his breast, then pushed him from him, when the door was thrown wide open.

It was the landlord and the Auvergnat, who brought the police. Jean François sprang forward to the landing-place, held out his hands for the handcuffs, and said, laughing, " Forward, bad lot ! "

To-day he is at Cayenne, condemned for life as an incorrigible.

THE ATTACK ON THE MILL

BY

EMILE ZOLA

From " Jacques Damour," by Emile Zola.   Translated
by William Foster Apthorp.   Published by
Copeland & Day.

THE ATTACK ON THE MILL

BY EMILE ZOLA

I.

OLD Merlier's mill was in high feather, that fine summer evening. In the courtyard they had set out three tables, end to end, ready for the guests. All the country knew that, on that day, Merlier's daughter Françoise was to be betrothed to Dominique, a fellow who had the name of being an idle loafer, but whom the women for eight miles round looked at with glistening eyes, so well-favored was he.

This mill of old Merlier's was a real delight. It stood just in the middle of Rocreuse, at the point where the highway makes a sharp turn. The village has only one street, two rows of hovels, one row on each side of the road; but there, at the corner, the fields spread out wide, great trees, following the course of the Morelle, cover the depths of the valley with a magnificent shade. There is not in all Lorraine a more lovely bit of nature. To the right and left, thick woods of century-old trees rise up the gentle slopes, fill-ing the horizon with a sea of verdure; while, towards the south, the plain stretches out marvellously fertile, unfolding without end its plots of land divided by live hedges. But what, above all else, gives Rocreuse its charm is the coolness of this green nook in the hottest days of July and August. The Morelle comes down from the Gagny woods, and it seems as if it brought with it the coolness of the foliage beneath which it flows for miles; it brings the murmuring sounds, the icy and sequestered shade of the forests. And it is not the only source of coolness: all sorts of running water babble beneath the trees; at every step springs gush forth; you feel, while following the narrow paths, as if subterranean lakes were forcing their way through the moss, and taking advantage of the smallest fissures, at the foot of trees, between rocks, to overflow in crystalline fountains. The whispering voices of these brooks rise so multitudinous and high that they drown the bulfinches' song. You would think yourself in some enchanted park, with waterfalls on every hand.

Below, the meadows are soaking wet. Gigantic chestnuts cast their black shadows. Along the edge of the fields, long lines of poplars spread out their rustling drapery. There are two avenues of huge sycamore-maples rising across the fields, up toward the old château of Gagny, now in ruins. In this perpetually watered soil the

weeds grow rank. It is like a flower garden lying
between two wooded hillsides; but a natural garden, in which the lawns are fields, and giant trees
trace out colossal flower-beds. When the sun,
at noon, casts its rays straight down, the shadows
turn blue, the scorched weeds slumber in the
heat, while an icy shudder runs along beneath
the foliage.

It was there that old Merlier's mill enlivened a
nook of rank green growth with its clacking. The
building, of planks and mortar, seemed as old as
the world. Half of it dipped into the Morelle,
which, at this point, widens out into a clear,
rounded basin. A dam was contrived to let the
water fall from a height of several metres upon
the mill-wheel, which turned creaking, with the
asthmatic cough of a faithful servant, grown old
in the household. When people advised old
Merlier to change it for a new one, he would
shake his head, saying that a young wheel would
be lazier and not so well up in its business; and
he mended the old one with everything that came
to hand,—staves of casks, bits of rusty iron, zinc,
lead. The wheel seemed all the gayer for it, its
outline grown strange, all beplumed with weeds
and moss. When the water beat against it with
its silver stream, it would cover itself with beads,
you saw it deck out its strange carcass with a
sparkling bedizenment of mother-of-pearl neck-
laces.

The part of the mill that thus dipped into the
Morelle looked like a barbarous ark, stranded
there. A good half of the structure was built on
piles. The water ran in under the board floor;
there, too, were holes, well known in the country
for the eels and enormous crawfish caught there.
Above the fall, the basin was as clear as a mirror,
and when the wheel did not cloud it with its foam,
you could see shoals of large fish swimming there
with the deliberateness of a naval squadron. A
broken flight of steps led down to the river, near
a stake to which a boat was moored. A wooden
balcony ran above the wheel. Windows opened
upon it, cut at irregular distances. This pellmell
of corners, little walls, L's added as an after-
thought, beams and bits of roof, gave the mill
the appearance of an old dismantled citadel.
But ivy had grown there, all sorts of climbing
vines had stopped up the two wide cracks and
thrown a cloak of green over the old dwelling.
Young ladies who passed by would sketch old
Merlier's mill in their albums.

Toward the road the house was stouter. A
stone gateway opened upon the main courtyard,
which was bordered on the right by sheds and
stables. Near a well a huge elm covered half
the courtyard with its shade. At the farther
end, the house showed the line of its four first-
story windows, surmounted by a pigeon-house.
Old Merlier's only bit of dandyism was to have

this wall whitewashed every ten years. It had just been whitened, and dazzled the village when the sun lighted it up in the middle of the day.

For twenty years old Merlier had been mayor of Rocreuse. He was esteemed for the fortune he had managed to make. He was supposed to be worth something like eighty thousand francs, laid up sou by sou. When he married Madeleine Guillard, who brought him the mill as her dowry, he hardly possessed anything but his two arms; but Madeleine never repented her choice, so well did he manage the affairs of the household. Now that his wife was dead, he remained a widower with his daughter Françoise. No doubt, he might have taken a rest, left his mill to sleep in the moss; but he would have been too much bored, and the house would have seemed dead to him. He kept on working, for the fun of it. Old Merlier was then a tall old man, with a long, silent face, never laughing, but very jolly internally, nevertheless. He had been chosen for mayor on account of his money, and also for the fine air he knew how to assume, when he married a couple.

Françoise Merlier was just eighteen. She did not pass for one of the beauties of the country-side; she was too puny. Up to the age of eleven she was even ugly. No one in Rocreuse could understand how the daughter of father and mother Merlier, both of them ruggedly built,

could grow up so ill, and, so to speak, grudgingly.
But at fifteen, although still delicate, she had the
prettiest little face in the world.   She had black
hair, black eyes, and at the same time was all
rosy ; a mouth that laughed all the time, dimpled
cheeks, a clear brow on which there seemed to
rest a crown of sunshine.   Although puny for the
neighborhood, she was not thin, far from it ; people only meant that she could not shoulder a sack
of grain ; but she grew very plump with time,
and stood a good chance of ending by being round
and dainty as a quail.   Only her father's long
spells of speechlessness had made her thoughtful at an early age.   If she was always laughing,
it was to give others pleasure.   At bottom, she
was serious.

Naturally all the countryside courted her, still
more for her dollars than for her niceness.   And
at last, she made a choice that had just scandalized the country.   On the other side of the Morelle lived a young fellow, named Dominique
Penquer.   He did not belong in Rocreuse.   Ten
years before, he had come there from Belgium,
to take possession of a legacy from an uncle of
his who owned a little piece of property on the
very outskirts of the Gagny forest, just opposite
the mill, within a few gunshots.   He came to sell
this property, he said, and go home again.   But
the country fascinated him, it seems, for he did
not stir.   He was seen tilling his bit of field,

picking a few vegetables, on which he lived. He fished, he went shooting; several times the gamekeepers just missed catching him and reporting him to the authorities. This free life, the material resources of which the peasants could not well account for, had at last given him a bad name. He was vaguely spoken of as a poacher. At all events, he was lazy, for he was often found asleep in the grass at times when he ought to have been at work. The hut in which he lived, under the first trees of the forest, did not look like an honest fellow's dwelling either. If he had had business with the wolves of the old ruins of Gagny, it would not have surprised the old women. Yet the girls would, now and then, have the audacity to stand up for him; for this suspicious man was a superb fellow, tall and supple as a poplar, with a very white skin, and fair beard and hair that shone like gold in the sun. So, one fine morning, Françoise declared to her father that she loved Dominique, and that she would never consent to marry any one else.

You can imagine what a blow old Merlier received that day. He said nothing, as usual. He always looked thoughtful in the face; only his internal jollity stopped sparkling in his eyes. The two did not speak for a week. Françoise, too, was very grave. What bothered old Merlier was to make out how in the world that rascal of a

poacher could have bewitched his daughter.
Dominique had never come to the mill. The
miller began to watch him, and espied the gallant
on the other side of the Morelle, lying in the grass
and pretending to be asleep. The thing was
clear: they must have fallen in love, making
sheep's-eyes at each other across the mill-wheel.

Meanwhile another week passed by. Françoise looked more and more solemn. Old Merlier still said nothing. Then, one evening, he
brought Dominique home with him, without a
word. Françoise was just setting the table. She
did not seem astonished; she only added another plate and knife and fork; but the little
dimples appeared once more in her cheeks, and
her laugh came back again. That morning old
Merlier had gone after Dominique to his hut on
the outskirts of the wood. There the two men
had talked for three hours, with closed doors and
windows. No one ever knew what they found to
say to each other. What was certain was that,
on coming out, old Merlier already treated Dominique like his own son. No doubt, the old man
had found the man he was after, a fine fellow, in
this lazybones who lay in the grass to make the
girls fall in love with him.

All Rocreuse gossiped. The women, in the
doorways, did not run dry of tittle-tattle about
old Merlier's folly in taking a scapegrace into his
household. He let them talk on. Perhaps he

remembered his own marriage. Neither had he a red sou when he married Madeleine and her mill; but that did not prevent his making a good husband. Besides, Dominique cut the gossip short by going to work with such a will that the whole country marvelled at it. It so happened that the miller's boy had just been drafted; and Dominique would never hear of his hiring another. He carried the sacks, drove the cart, struggled with the old wheel when it had to be begged hard before it would turn, and all with such a will that people would come to look at him for sheer pleasure. Old Merlier laughed his quiet laugh. He was very proud of having scented out this fellow. There is nothing like love for putting heart into young people.

In the midst of all this hard work Françoise and Dominique adored each other. They hardly ever spoke, but they looked at each other with smiling tenderness. So far, old Merlier had not said a single word about the marriage; and they both respected this silence, awaiting the old man's pleasure. At last, one day about the middle of July, he had three tables set out in the courtyard under the big elm, inviting his friends in Rocreuse to come and take a drink with him in the evening. When the courtyard was full, and every one had his glass in his hand, old Merlier raised his very high, saying:

—— "This is for the pleasure of announcing to

you that Françoise will marry that fellow there in a month, on Saint-Louis's day."

Then they clinked glasses noisily. Everybody laughed. But old Merlier, raising his voice, went on,—

—— "Dominique, kiss your intended. That must be done."

And they kissed each other, very red, while the crowd laughed still louder. It was a real jollification. A small cask was emptied. Then, when only the intimate friends were left, they chatted quietly. Night had come, a starlit and very clear night. Dominique and Françoise, sitting side by side on a bench, said nothing. An old peasant spoke of the war the emperor had declared with Prussia. All the boys in the village were already gone. The day before, troops had passed through. There would be hard knocks going.

—— "Bah!" said old Merlier, with a happy man's egoism. "Dominique is a foreigner, he won't go. . . . And, if the Prussians come, he will be here to defend his wife."

This notion that the Prussians might come seemed a good joke. They were to be given an A 1 thrashing, and it would be soon over.

—— "I've seen 'em, I've seen 'em," the old peasant said over and over again.

There was a silence. Then they clinked glasses once more. Françoise and Dominique had heard nothing; they had taken each other softly by the hand, behind the bench, so that no one could see them, and it seemed so good that they stayed there, their eyes lost in the depths of the darkness.

How warm and splendid a night! The village was falling asleep on both sides of the road, tranquil as a child. You only heard, from time to time, the crowing of some cock, waked too soon. From the great woods hard by came long breaths that passed like caresses over the roofs. The meadows, with their black shadows, put on a mysterious and secluded majesty, while all the running waters that gushed forth into the darkness seemed to be the cool and rhythmic breathing of the sleeping country. At moments, the mill-wheel, fast asleep, seemed to be dreaming, like those old watchdogs that bark while snoring. It creaked, it talked all by itself, lulled by the falls of the Morelle, whose sheet of water gave forth the sustained and musical note of an organ pipe. Never had more widespread peace fallen over a happier corner of the earth.

II.

JUST a month later, day for day, on Saint-Louis's eve, Rocreuse was in dismay. The Prussians had beaten the emperor, and were advancing toward the village by forced marches. For

a week past, people passing along the road had
announced the Prussians: "They are at Lor-
mière, they are at Novelles;" and, hearing that
they were approaching so fast, Rocreuse thought,
every morning, to see them come down by the
Gagny woods. Still, they did not come; this
frightened the inhabitants still more. They
would surely fall upon the village at night and
cut everybody's throat.

The night before, a little before daybreak,
there had been an alarm. The inhabitants had
waked up, hearing a great noise of men on the
road. The women were just falling upon their
knees and crossing themselves, when red trousers were recognized through cracks of windows
prudently opened. It was a detachment of
French. The captain immediately asked for the
mayor of the place, and stayed at the mill, after
talking with old Merlier.

The sun rose gayly that day. It would be hot
at noon. Over the woods floated a yellow light,
while in the distance, above the meadows, rose
white vapors. The clean, pretty village awoke
in the cool air, and the country, with its river
and springs, had the dew-sprinkled loveliness of
a nosegay. But this fine weather made no one
laugh. They had just seen the captain walk
round about the mill, examine the neighboring
houses, cross to the other side of the Morelle,
and from there study the country through a spy-

glass; old Merlier, who was with him, seemed to
be explaining the country to him. Then the captain stationed soldiers behind walls, behind trees,
in holes in the ground. The bulk of the detachment was encamped in the courtyard of the mill.
So there was to be a fight? And when old Merlier came back, he was plied with questions. He
gave a long nod with his head, without speaking.
Yes, there was to be a fight.

Françoise and Dominique were in the courtyard, looking at him. At last, he took his pipe
out of his mouth and said simply,—

—— "Ah! my poor children, there will be no
wedding for you to-morrow!"

Dominique, his lips set, a line of anger across
his forehead, raised himself up on tiptoe from time
to time, with his eyes fixed on the Gagny woods,
as if he longed to see the Prussians come. Françoise, very pale, serious, came and went, supply-
ing the soldiers with what they needed. They
were making their soup in a corner of the courtyard, and joking while waiting for their meal.

Meanwhile the captain seemed delighted. He
had examined the rooms and the great hall of
the mill, looking out upon the river. Now, sitting by the well, he was talking with old Merlier.

—— "You have a real fortress here," said he.
"We ought to hold out till evening. . . . The beggars are late. They should be here by this time."

The miller looked serious. He saw his mill

flaming like a torch; but he did not complain, thinking it useless. He only opened his mouth to say,—

—— "You ought to have some one hide the boat behind the wheel. There is a hole there that will hold her. . . . Perhaps she may be of use."

The captain gave an order. This captain was a handsome man of about forty, tall and with a kindly face. The sight of Françoise and Dominique seemed to please him. He was interested in them, as if he had forgotten the coming struggle. He followed Françoise about with his eyes, and his look told plainly that he found her charming. Then, turning to Dominique,—

—— "So you 're not in the army, my boy?" he asked abruptly.

—— "I 'm a foreigner," the young man answered.

The captain seemed only half pleased with this reason. He winked and smiled. Françoise was pleasanter company than cannon. Then, seeing him smile, Dominique added,—

—— "I 'm a foreigner, but I can put a bullet into an apple at five hundred metres. . . . See, my gun 's there, behind you."

—— "It may be of use to you," the captain replied simply.

Françoise had come up, trembling a little. And, without minding the people there, Dominique took both the hands she held out to him, and pressed them in his, as if to take her under his protection. The captain smiled again, but added not a word. He remained sitting, his sword between his legs, his eyes looking at vacancy, as if in a dream.

It was already two o'clock. It was growing very hot. There was a dead silence. In the courtyard, under the sheds, the soldiers had fallen to eating their soup. Not a sound came from the village, in which the people had barricaded their houses, doors, and windows. A dog, left alone in the road, was howling. From the neighboring woods and meadows, motionless in the heat, came a far-off voice, long sustained, made up of every separate breath of air. A cuckoo was singing. Then the silence spread itself over the country also.

And, in this slumbering air, a shot suddenly burst forth. The captain sprang up quickly, the soldiers dropped their plates of soup, still half full. In a few seconds, every man was at his post for the fight; the mill was occupied from top to bottom. Yet the captain, who had gone out upon the road, could make out nothing; to the right and left, the road stretched out, empty and all white. A second shot was heard, and still nothing, not a shadow; but, on turning round, he espied, over towards Gagny, between two trees, a light cloudlet of smoke wafted away like gossamer. The wood was still profoundly quiet.

—— " The rascals have taken to the forest," he muttered. " They know we are here."

Then the firing kept up harder, and harder, between the French soldiers, stationed round the mill, and the Prussians, hidden behind the trees. The bullets whistled across the Morelle, without occasioning any loss on one side or the other. The shots were irregular, came from every bush; and all you saw was still the little clouds of smoke gently wafted away by the wind. This lasted for nearly two hours. The officer hummed a tune, as if indifferent. Françoise and Dominique, who had stayed in the courtyard, raised themselves up on tiptoe, and looked over the wall. They were particularly interested in watching a little soldier, stationed on the brink of the Morelle, behind the hulk of an old boat; he was flat on his belly, watched his chance, fired his shot, then let himself slide down into a ditch, a little behind him, to reload his rifle; and his movements were so droll, so cunning, so supple, that it made one smile to see him. He must have espied the head of some Prussian, for he got up quickly and brought his piece to his shoulder; but, before he fired, he gave a cry, turned over upon himself, and rolled into the ditch, where his legs stiffened out with the momentary, convulsive jerk of those of a chicken with its neck wrung. The little soldier had received a bullet full in the breast. He was the first man killed. Instinctively Françoise seized hold of Dominique's hand and squeezed it with a nervous grip.

—— "Don't stay there," said the captain. "The bullets reach here."

As he spoke a little, sharp stroke was heard in the old elm, and a branch fell in zigzags through the air; but the two young people did not stir, riveted there by anxiety at the sight On the outskirts of the wood, a Prussian came out suddenly from behind a tree, as from a side scene, beating the air with his arms, and tumbling over backwards. And then nothing stirred, the two dead men seemed to sleep in the dazzling sunshine, you saw no one in the torpid landscape. Even the crack of the shots stopped. Only the Morelle kept up its silver-toned whispering.

Old Merlier looked at the captain in surprise, as if to ask if it were over.

—— "Here it comes," the latter muttered. "Look out! Don't stay there."

He had not finished speaking when there came a terrific volley. It was as if the great elm were mowed down, a cloud of leaves whirled about them. Luckily the Prussians had fired too high. Dominique dragged, almost carried Françoise away, while old Merlier followed them, crying out,—

4

—— "Go down to the little cellar; the walls
are solid."

But they did not mind him, they went into the
great hall, where ten soldiers, or so, were waiting in silence, with shutters closed, peeping
through the cracks. The captain had stayed
alone in the courtyard, crouched down behind
the little wall, while the furious volleys continued. The soldiers he had stationed outside
yielded ground only foot by foot. Yet they
came in, one by one, crawling on their faces,
when the enemy had dislodged them from their
hiding-places. Their orders were to gain time,
not to show themselves, so that the Prussians
might not know what numbers they had before
them. Another hour went by; and, as a sergeant came up, saying that there were only two
or three men left outside, the officer looked at his
watch, muttering,——

—— "Half after two. . . . Come, we must
hold out four hours."

He had the gate of the courtyard shut, and all
preparations were made for an energetic resist-
ance. As the Prussians were on the other side
of the Morelle, an immediate assault was not to
be feared. To be sure, there was a bridge, a
little over a mile off, but they doubtless did not
know of its existence, and it was hardly probable
that they would try to ford the river. So the
officer merely had the road watched. The whole

effort was to be made on the side toward the fields.

The firing had once more ceased. The mill seemed dead beneath the hot sun. Not a shutter was opened, not a sound came from the inside. Little by little, meanwhile, the Prussians showed themselves at the outskirts of the Gagny wood. They stretched forth their heads, grew more daring. In the mill, several soldiers had already levelled their rifles; but the captain cried out,—

—— "No, no, wait. . . . Let them come up."

They were very cautious about it, looking at the mill with evident distrust. This old dwelling, silent and dismal, with its curtains of ivy made them uneasy. Still, they kept advancing. When there were about fifty of them in the meadow opposite, the officer said a single word,—

—— "Fire!"

A tearing sound was heard, followed by single shots. Françoise, shaken with a fit of trembling, put her hands up to her ears, in spite of herself. Dominique, behind the soldiers, looked on; and, when the smoke had blown away a little, he saw three Prussians stretched on their backs in the middle of the field. The rest had thrown themselves down behind the willows and poplars; and the siege began.

For over an hour the mill was riddled with bullets. They whipped its old walls like hail.

When they struck stone, you heard them flatten
out and fall back into the water.   Into wood they
penetrated with a hollow sound.   Now and then
a cracking told that the wheel had been hit.   The
soldiers inside husbanded their shots, fired only
when they could take aim.   From time to time
the captain would look at his watch; and, as a
ball split a shutter and then lodged in the ceiling,—

—— "Four o'clock," he muttered.   "We shall
never hold out."

It was true, this terrible firing of musketry
was shivering the old mill.   A shutter fell into
the water, riddled like a piece of lace, and had to
be replaced by a mattress.   Old Merlier exposed
himself every moment, to make sure of the in-
jury done to his poor wheel, whose cracking went
to his heart.   It was all over with it, this time;
never would he be able to repair it.   Dominique
had implored Françoise to go, but she would
stay with him; she had sat down behind a great
oak clothespress, the sides of which gave out a
deep sound.   Then Dominique placed himself
in front of Françoise.   He had not fired yet; he
held his gun in his hands, not being able to get
up to the windows, whose entire width was taken
up by the soldiers.   At every discharge the floor
shook.

—— "Look out! look out!" the captain cried
of a sudden.

He had just seen a whole black mass come out from the wood. Immediately a formidable platoon fire was opened. It was as if a water-spout had passed over the mill. Another shutter gave way, and, by the gaping opening of the window, the bullets came in. Two soldiers rolled upon the floor. One did not move; they pushed him up against the wall, because he was in the way. The other squirmed on the ground, begging them to make an end of him; but no one minded him, the balls kept coming in, every one shielded himself, and tried to find a loophole to fire back through. A third soldier was wounded; he said not a word, he let himself slide down by the edge of a table, with fixed and haggard eyes. Opposite these dead men, Françoise, seized with horror, had pushed her chair aside mechanically, to sit down on the ground next the wall; she felt smaller there, and in less danger. Meanwhile they had gone after all the mattresses in the house, and had half stopped up the window. The hall was getting filled with rubbish, with broken weapons, with gutted furniture.

—— "Five o'clock," said the captain. "Keep it up. . . . They are going to try to cross the water."

At this instant Françoise gave a shriek. A rebounding ball had just grazed her forehead. A few drops of blood appeared. Dominique looked at her; then, stepping up to the window, he fired his first shot, and kept on firing. He loaded, fired, without paying any attention to what was going on near him; only from time to time he would give Françoise a look. For the rest, he did not hurry himself, took careful aim. The Prussians, creeping along by the poplars, were attempting the passage of the Morelle, as the captain had foreseen; but, as soon as one of them risked showing himself, he would fall, hit in the head by a ball from Dominique. The captain, who followed this game, was astonished. He complimented the young man, saying that he would be glad to have a lot of marksmen like him. Dominique did not hear him. A ball cut his shoulder, another bruised his arm; and he kept on firing.

There were two more men killed. The matresses, all slashed to bits, no longer stopped up the windows. A last volley seemed as if it would carry away the mill. The position was no longer tenable. Still the officer repeated,—

—— " Stick to it. . . . Half an hour more."

Now he counted the minutes. He had promised his superior officers to hold the enemy there until evening, and would not draw back a sole's breadth before the time he had set for the retreat. He still had his gracious manner, smiling at Françoise, to reassure her. He himself had just picked up a dead soldier's rifle, and was firing.

There were only four soldiers left in the hall.
The Prussians showed themselves in a body on
the other bank of the Morelle, and it was evident
that they might cross the river at any time. A
few minutes more elapsed. The captain stuck
to it obstinately, would not give the order to
retreat, when a sergeant came running up, saying,—

—— " They are on the road, they are going to
take us in the rear."

The Prussians must have found the bridge.
The captain pulled out his watch.

—— " Five minutes more," said he. " They
won't be here for five minutes."

Then, at the stroke of six, he at last consented
to order his men out by a little door, opening
upon an alleyway. From there they threw themselves into a ditch, they reached the Sauval forest.
Before going, the captain saluted old Merlier
very politely, excusing himself. And he even
added,—

—— " Make them lose time. . . . We shall be
back again."

Meanwhile Dominique stayed on in the hall.
He still kept firing, hearing nothing, understanding nothing. He only felt that he must defend
Françoise. The soldiers were gone, without his
suspecting it the least in the world. He took aim
and killed his man at every shot. Suddenly
there was a loud noise. The Prussians, from

the rear, had just overrun the courtyard. He
fired his last shot, and they fell upon him as his
piece was still smoking.

Four men held him. Others shouted round
him in a frightful language. They all but cut his
throat off-hand. Françoise threw herself before
him in supplication ; but an officer came in and
took charge of the prisoner. After a few sen-
tences exchanged in German with the soldiers, he
turned to Dominique and said roughly, and in
very good French,—

—— " You will be shot in two hours."

III.

It was a rule made by the German staff : every
Frenchman not belonging to the regular army,
and taken with arms in his hands, should be shot.
Even the guerilla companies were not recognized
as belligerents. By thus making terrible exam-
ples of the peasants who defended their own
firesides, the Germans wished to prevent the
uprising of the whole country en masse, which
they dreaded.

The officer, a tall, lean man of about fifty,
put Dominique through a brief examination.
Although he spoke very pure French, he had
quite the Prussian stiffness.

—— " You belong in these parts ? "

—— " No, I am a Belgian."

—— " Why have you taken up arms? . . .
All this can't be any of your business."

Dominique did not answer. At this moment,
the officer caught sight of Françoise, standing
upright and very pale, listening ; her slight wound
put a red bar across her white forehead. He
looked at the young people, one after the other,
seemed to understand, and contented himself
with adding,——

—— " You don't deny that you were firing? "

—— " I fired as long as I was able," Dominique answered quietly.

This confession was needless, for he was black
with powder, covered with sweat, spotted with
some drops of blood that had run down from the
scratch on his shoulder.

—— " Very well," the officer repeated. " You
will be shot in two hours."

Françoise did not cry out. She clasped her
hands together and raised them in a gesture of
mute despair. The officer noticed this gesture.
Two soldiers had led Dominique away into the
next room, where they were to keep him in sight.
The young girl had dropped down upon a chair,
her legs giving way under her ; she could not cry,
she was choking. Meanwhile the officer kept
looking at her closely. At last he spoke to
her.

—— " That young man is your brother? " he
asked.

She shook her head. He stood there stiff, without a smile. Then, after a silence,—

—— "He has lived a long while in these parts?"

She nodded yes, still dumb.

—— "Then he must know the woods round here very well?"

This time she spoke.

—— "Yes, sir," she said, looking at him in some surprise.

He said no more, and turned on his heel, asking to have the mayor of the village brought to him. But Françoise had risen, a faint blush on her face, thinking to have caught the drift of his questions, and seeing fresh hope in them. It was she who ran to find her father.

Old Merlier, as soon as the shots had ceased, had run quickly down the wooden steps to look at his wheel. He adored his daughter, he had a stout friendship for Dominique, his intended son-in-law; but his wheel also held a large place in his heart. As the two young ones, as he called them, had come safe and sound out of the scrimmage, he thought of his other love, and this one had suffered grievously. And, bending over the huge wooden carcass, he investigated its wounds, the picture of distress. Five paddles were in splinters, the central framework was riddled. He stuck his fingers into the bullet holes, to measure their depth; he thought over how he could repair all this damage. Françoise found him already stopping up cracks with broken bits of wood and moss.

—— "Father," she said, "you are wanted."

And at last she wept, telling him what she had just heard. Old Merlier shook his head. You didn't shoot people that way. He must see. And he went back into the mill, with his silent, pacific air. When the officer asked him for victuals for his men, he answered that the people in Rocreuse were not accustomed to being bullied, and that nothing would be got from them by violence. He took everything upon himself, but on the condition of being allowed to act alone. The officer showed signs, at first, of getting angry at this cool manner; then he gave in to the old man's curt and businesslike way of talking. He even called him back, to ask him,——

—— "What do you call those woods there, opposite?"

—— "The Sauval woods."

—— "And what is their extent?"

The miller looked at him fixedly.

—— "I don't know," he answered.

And he walked away. An hour later the contributions of victuals and money required by the officer were in the courtyard of the mill. Night was approaching; Françoise followed the soldiers' movements anxiously. She did not go far from the room in which Dominique was shut up. At

about seven she had a poignant emotion; she
saw the officer go into the prisoner's room, and,
for a quarter of an hour, she heard their voices
raised. One instant, the officer reappeared on
the threshold, to give an order in German, which
she did not understand; but, when twelve men
came and fell into line in the courtyard, with
their muskets, she fell a-trembling, she felt ready
to die. So it was all over; the execution was to
take place. The twelve men waited there ten
minutes. Dominique's voice was still raised in
a tone of violent refusal. At last the officer
came out, slamming the door and saying,—

—— "Very well, think it over. . . . I give
you till to-morrow morning."

And, with a motion of his arm, he ordered the
twelve men to break ranks. Françoise stayed on
in a sort of stupor. Old Merlier, who had not
stopped smoking his pipe, while looking at the
squad with an air of simple curiosity, came up
and took her by the arm with fatherly gentleness.
He led her to her room.

—— "Keep quiet," he said, " try to sleep. . . .
To-morrow it will be daylight, and we will see."

When he withdrew, he locked her in, for pru-
dence sake. It was a principle of his that women
were no good, and that they made a mess of it
whenever they undertook anything serious. But
Françoise did not go to bed; she stayed a long
time sitting on her bed, listening to the noises in

the house. The German soldiers, encamped in the
courtyard, were singing and laughing: they must
have been eating and drinking up to eleven, for the
noise did not stop for an instant. In the mill
itself heavy steps sounded every now and then;
no doubt, they were relieving sentries. But what
interested her, above all, were noises that she
could not make out, in the room under hers.
Several times she lay down on the ground, she
put her ear to the floor. This room happened to
be the one in which Dominique was locked up.
He must have been walking from the wall to the
window, for she long heard the regular cadence
of his steps; then there was a dead silence, he
had doubtless sat down. Besides, the noises
stopped, everything was hushed in sleep. When
the house seemed to her to slumber, she opened
the window as softly as possible, and rested her
elbows on the sill.

Outside, the night was calm and warm. The
slender crescent moon, setting behind the Sauval
woods, lighted up the country with the glimmer
of a night taper. The elongated shadows of the
great trees barred the meadows with black, while
the grass, in the unshaded spots, put on the soft-
ness of greenish velvet. But Françoise did not
stop to note the mysterious charm of the night.
She examined the country, looking for the sentinels that the Germans must have stationed on
one side. She plainly saw their shadows, ranged

like the rungs of a ladder along the Morelle.
Only a single one stood opposite the mill, on the
other side of the river near a willow whose
branches dipped into the water. Françoise saw
him distinctly; he was a big fellow, standing
motionless, his face turned toward the sky with
the dreamy look of a shepherd.

Then, when she had carefully inspected the
ground, she went back and sat down upon her
bed. She stayed there an hour deeply absorbed.
Then she listened again; in the house not a
breath stirred. She went back to the window,
and looked out; but, no doubt, she saw danger
in one of the horns of the moon, which still appeared behind the trees, for she went back again
to wait. At last the time seemed to have come.
The night was quite dark, she no longer saw the
sentinel opposite, the country lay spread out like
a pool of ink. She listened intently for a moment, and made up her mind. An iron ladder
ran near the window, some bars let into the wall,
leading from the wheel up to the loft, down which
the millers used to climb, to get at certain cog-
wheels; then, when the machinery had been
altered, the ladder had long since disappeared
beneath the rank growth of ivy that covered that
side of the mill.

Françoise bravely climbed over the balustrade
of her window, grasped one of the iron bars,
and found herself in empty space. She began

to climb down. Her skirts were much in her way. Suddenly a stone broke loose from the masonry, and fell into the Morelle with a re-sounding splash. She stopped, chilled with a shudder. But she saw that the waterfall, with its continuous roar, drowned out from afar any noise she might make, and she climbed down more boldly, feeling for the ivy with her foot, making sure of the rungs of the ladder. When she had got on a level with the room that was used as Dominique's prison, she stopped. An unforeseen difficulty nearly made her lose all her courage ; the window of the room below was not cut regularly under the window of her chamber ; it was some way from the ladder, and, when she stretched out her hand, she felt only the wall. Would she have to climb up again, without carrying her plan through to the end? Her arms were getting tired, the murmur of the Morelle beneath her began to make her dizzy. Then she tore off little bits of mortar from the wall, and threw them against Dominique's win-dow. He did not hear, perhaps he was asleep. She broke off some more pieces from the wall, barking her fingers. And her strength was giving out, she felt herself falling backwards, when Dominique, at last, softly opened his window.

—— "It's I," she whispered. "Take me quick, I'm falling."

It was the first time she had tutoyéed him. He caught her, leaning out, and lifted her into the room. There she had a fit of tears stifling her sobs, so as not to be heard. Then, by a supreme effort, she calmed herself.

—— "You are guarded?" she asked, in a low voice.

Dominique, still dumfounded at seeing her thus, made a simple sign, pointing to his door. They heard a snoring on the other side; the sentinel must have given way to drowsiness, and lain down on the ground, across the doorway, thinking that, in this way, the prisoner could not get out.

—— "You must run away," she went on rapidly. "I have come to implore you to run away, and to say good-bye."

But he did not seem to hear her. He kept repeating :

—— "How, it's you, it's you! . . . how you frightened me! You might have killed yourself."

He took her hands, he kissed them.

—— "How I love you, Françoise! . . . You are as brave as you are good. I only had one fear, that of dying without seeing you once more. . . . But you are here, and now they can shoot me. When I have had a quarter of an hour with you I shall be ready."

Little by little he had drawn her closer to him, and she rested her head upon his shoulder.

The danger drew them nearer together.   They forgot all in this embrace.

—— "Ah! Françoise," Dominique went on, in a caressing voice, " to-day is Saint-Louis's day, our wedding day, that we have waited for so long.   Nothing has been able to separate us, since we are here, all alone, faithful to our tryst. . . .   It's our wedding morning now, is n't it ? "

—— " Yes, yes," she repeated, " our wedding morning."

They exchanged a kiss, trembling.   But of a sudden she broke loose, the terrible reality rose up before her.

—— " You must run away, you must run away," she stammered out.   " Let us not lose a minute."

And, as he stretched out his arms once more to take her in the darkness, she again tutoyéed him,—

—— " Oh ! I beg you, listen to me. . . .   If you die, I shall die.   In an hour it will be daylight. I wish you to go at once."

Then, rapidly, she explained her plan.   The iron ladder ran down to the wheel : there, he could take the paddles and get into the boat which was in a recess.   After that it would be easy for him to reach the other bank of the river and escape.

—— " But there must be sentinels there ? " he said.

" Only one, opposite, at the foot of the first willow."

5

—— " And if he sees me, if he tries calling out ? "

Françoise shuddered.   She put a knife she had brought down with her into his hand.   There was a silence.

—— " And your father, and you ? " Dominique continued.   " But no, I can't run away. . . . When I am gone, maybe these soldiers will slaughter you. . . . You don't know them. They proposed to show me mercy, if I would be their guide through the Sauval forest.   When they find me gone they will stick at nothing."

The young girl did not stop to discuss.   She simply answered all the reasons he gave with,—

—— " For the love of me, fly. . . . If you love me, Dominique, don't stay here a minute longer."

Then she promised to climb back to her room. They would not know that she had helped him. She at last took him in her arms, kissed him to convince him, in an extraordinary outburst of passion.   He was beaten.   He asked not a question further.

—— " Swear to me that your father knows of what you are doing, and that he advises me to run away ? "

—— " It was my father sent me," Françoise answered boldly.

She lied.   At this moment she felt nothing but a boundless need of knowing him in safety, of escaping from this abominable thought that the

sun would give the signal for his death. When
he was gone, all mishaps might rush down upon
her; it would seem sweet to her, as long as he
was alive. The selfishness of her love wished
him alive, before all else.

—— "Very well," said Dominique, "I will do
as you please."

Then they said nothing more. Dominique
went to open the window again; but suddenly
a noise chilled their blood. The door was
shaken, and they thought it was being opened.
Evidently a patrol had heard their voices; and
both of them, standing pressed against each
other, waited in unspeakable anguish. The door
was shaken again, but it did not open. Each
gave a stifled sigh; they saw how it was, it must
have been the soldier lying across the threshold
turning over. And really, silence was restored,
the snoring began again.

Dominique would have it that Françoise must
first climb back to her room. He took her in his
arms; he bade her a mute farewell. Then he
helped her to seize the ladder, and grappled hold
of it in his turn. But he refused to go down a
single rung before he knew she was in her
room. When Françoise had climbed in, she
whispered, in a voice light as a breath,—

—— "Au revoir; I love you!"

She stopped with her elbows resting on the
window-sill, and tried to follow Dominique with

her eyes. The night was still very dark. She
looked for the sentinel, and did not see him; only
the willow made a pale spot in the midst of the
darkness. For an instant she heard the rustling
of Dominique's body along the ivy. Then the
wheel creaked, and there was a gentle splashing
that told that the young man had found the boat.
A minute later, in fact, she made out the dark
outline of the boat on the gray sheet of the
Morelle. Then anguish stopped her breath. At
every moment she thought to hear the sentinel's
cry of alarm. The faintest sounds, scattered
through the darkness, seemed to be the hurried
tread of soldiers, the clatter of arms, the click
of the hammers on the rifles. Yet seconds
elapsed, the country slept on in sovereign peace.
Dominique must have been landing on the other
bank. Françoise saw nothing more. The stillness was majestic. And she heard a noise of
scuffling feet, a hoarse cry, the dull thud of a falling body. Then the silence grew deeper; and,
as if she had felt death passing by, she waited on,
all cold, face to face with the pitch-dark night.

IV.

At daybreak, shouting voices shook the mill.
Old Merlier had come to open Françoise's door.
She came down into the courtyard, pale and very
calm. But there she gave a shudder before the

dead body of a Prussian soldier, which was stretched out near the well, on a cloak spread on the ground.

Around the body, soldiers were gesticulating, crying aloud in fury. Many of them shook their fists at the village. Meanwhile, the officer had had old Merlier called, as mayor of the township.

—— " See here," said he, in a voice choking with rage, " here's one of our men who has been found murdered by the river-side. . . . We must make a tremendous example, and I trust you will help us to find out the murderer."

—— " Anything you please," answered the miller in his phlegmatic way. " Only it will not be easy."

The officer had stooped down to throw aside a flap of the cloak that hid the dead man's face. Then a horrible wound appeared. The sentinel had been struck in the throat, and the weapon was left in the wound. It was a kitchen knife with a black handle.

—— " Look at this knife," said the officer to old Merlier, " perhaps it may help us in our search."

The old man gave a start. But he recovered himself immediately, and answered, without moving a muscle of his face,—

—— " Everybody in these parts has knives like that. . . . Maybe your man was tired of fighting, and did the job himself. Such things have been known to happen."

—— "Shut up!" the officer cried furiously. "I don't know what keeps me from setting fire to the four corners of the village."

His anger luckily prevented his noticing the profound change that had come over Françoise's face. She had to sit down on the stone bench, near the well. In spite of herself her eyes never left that dead body, stretched on the ground almost at her feet. He was a big, handsome fellow, who looked like Dominique, with light hair and blue eyes. This resemblance made her heart sick. She thought of how the dead man had perhaps left some sweetheart behind, who would weep for him over there, in Germany. And she recognized her knife in the dead man's throat. She had killed him.

Meanwhile the officer talked of taking terrible measures against Rocreuse, when some soldiers came up running. They had only just noticed Dominique's escape. It occasioned an extreme agitation. The officer visited the premises, looked out of the window, which had been left open, understood it all, and came back exasperated.

Old Merlier seemed very much put out at Dominique's flight.

—— "The idiot!" he muttered, "he spoils it all."

Françoise, who heard him, was seized with anguish. For the rest, her father did not suspect her complicity. He shook his head, saying to her in an undertone,—

—— " Now we are in a fine scrape ! "

—— " It 's that rascal ! it 's that rascal ! " cried the officer. " He must have reached the woods. . . . But he must be found for us, or the village shall pay for it."

And, addressing the miller,—

—— " Come, you must know where he is hiding ? "

Old Merlier gave a noiseless chuckle, pointing to the wide extent of wooded hillside.

—— " How do you expect to find a man in there ? " said he.

—— " Oh ! there must be holes in there that you know of. I will give you ten men. You shall be their guide."

—— " All right. Only it will take us a week to beat all the woods in the neighborhood."

The old man's coolness infuriated the officer. In fact, he saw the ridiculousness of this battue. It was then that he caught sight of Françoise, pale and trembling, on the bench, The young girl's anxious attitude struck him. He said nothing for an instant, looking hard at the miller and Françoise by turns.

—— " Is n't this man," he at last brutally asked the old man, " your daughter's lover ? "

Old Merlier turned livid, and one would have thought him on the point of throwing himself upon the officer and strangling him. He drew himself up stiffly; he did not answer. Françoise put her face between her hands.

—— "Yes, that's it," the Prussian went on, "you or your daughter have helped him to run away. You are his accomplice. . . . For the last time, will you give him up to us?"

The miller did not answer, He had turned away, looking off into the distance, as if the officer had not been speaking to him. This put the last touch to the latter's anger.

—— "Very well," he said, "you shall be shot instead."

And he once more ordered out the firing party. Old Merlier still kept cool. He hardly gave a slight shrug of his shoulders; this whole drama seemed to him in rather bad taste. No doubt, he did not believe that a man was to be shot with so little ado. Then, when the squad had come, he said gravely:

—— "You're in earnest, then? . . . All right. If you absolutely must have some one, I will do as well as another."

But Françoise sprang up, half crazed, stammering out:

—— "Mercy, monsieur, don't do any harm to my father. Kill me instead. . . . It's I who helped Dominique to escape. I am the only culprit."

—— "Be quiet, little girl," cried old Merlier. "What are you lying for? . . . She spent the night locked up in her room, monsieur. She lies, I assure you."

—— "No, I am not lying," the young girl replied ardently. "I climbed down out of the window, I urged Dominique to fly. . . . It's the truth, the only truth. . . ."

The old man turned very pale. He saw clearly in her eyes that she was not lying, and this story appalled him. Ah! these children, with their hearts, how they spoiled everything! Then he grew angry.

—— "She's crazy, don't believe her. She is telling you stupid stories. . . . Come, let's have done with it."

She tried to protest again. She knelt down, she clasped her hands. The officer looked quietly on at this heartrending struggle.

—— "Good God!" he said at last, "I take your father, because I haven't got the other one. . . . Try and find the other one, and your father shall go free."

For a moment she looked at him, her eyes staring wide at the atrocity of this proposal.

—— "It's horrible," she murmured. "Where do you expect me to find Dominique at this time? He's gone; I don't know where he is."

—— "Well, choose. Him or your father."

—— "Oh! my God! how can I choose? But even if I knew where Dominique was, I could not choose! . . . It is my heart you are breaking.

. . . I had rather die at once. Yes, it would
be soonest over so. Kill me, I beg of you, kill
me. . . ."

The officer at last grew impatient at this scene
of despair and tears. He cried out,—

—— "I 've had enough of this! I 'm willing
to be good-natured, I consent to give you two
hours. . . . If your sweetheart is n't here in two
hours, your father shall pay for him."

And he had old Merlier taken to the room
which had been used for Dominique's prison.
The old man asked for some tobacco, and fell to
smoking. No emotion was to be detected in his
impassive face. Only, when he was alone, two
big tears ran slowly down his cheeks. His poor,
dear child ; how she suffered !

Françoise had stayed in the middle of the
courtyard. Some Prussian soldiers passed by,
laughing. Some of them called out to her, jokes
which she did not understand. She stared at
the door through which her father had just disappeared. And, with a slow movement, she
raised her hand to her forehead, as if to keep it
from bursting.

The officer turned on his heel, repeating :

—— "You have two hours. Try to make
good use of them."

She had two hours. This sentence kept buzzing in her head. Then, mechanically, she went
out of the courtyard, she walked straight before

her. Whither should she go? What should she
do? She did not even try to decide, because
she felt convinced of the uselessness of her efforts.
Yet she would have liked to find Dominique.
They would have come to an understanding together, they might perhaps have hit upon an
expedient. And, amid the confusion of her
thoughts, she went down to the bank of the
Morelle, which she crossed below the dam, at a
place where there were some large stones. Her
feet led her under the first willow, at the corner
of the field. As she bent down, she saw a pool
of blood that made her turn pale. That was
clearly the place. And she followed Dominique's tracks in the trodden grass; he must
have run, a line of long strides was to be seen
cutting through the field cornerwise. Then,
farther on, she lost the tracks; but, in a
neighboring field, she thought she found them
again. This brought her to the outskirts of
the forest, where all traces were wiped out.

Françoise plunged in under the trees, notwithstanding. It was a relief to be alone. She sat
down for a moment; then, remembering that
her time was running out, she got up again.
How long was it since she had left the mill?
Five minutes? half an hour? She had lost all
consciousness of time. Perhaps Dominique had
gone and hidden in a copse she knew of, where,
one afternoon, they had eaten filberts together.

She went to the copse and searched it. Only a
blackbird flew out, whistling its soft, melancholy
tune. Then she thought he had taken refuge in
a hollow in the rocks, where he sometimes used
to lie in ambush for game; but the hollow in the
rocks was empty. What was the use of looking
for him? she would not find him; and, little by
little, her desire to find him grew furious, she
walked on faster. The notion that he might
have climbed up a tree suddenly struck her.
From that moment she pushed on with up-
turned eyes, and, that he might know she was
near, she called out to him every fifteen or twenty
steps. The cuckoos answered her, a breath of
air passing through the branches made her think
he was there, and was coming down. Once she
even thought she saw him; she stopped, choking,
having a good mind to run away. What would
she say to him? Had she come, then, to lead
him away and have him shot? Oh! no, she
would not mention these things. She would cry
out to him to escape, not to stay in the neighborhood. Then the thought of her father waiting
for her gave her a sharp pang. She fell upon
the turf, weeping, repeating aloud,—

—— "My God! my God! why am I here?"

She was crazy to have come. And, as if
seized with fright, she ran, she tried to find a
way out of the forest. Three times she took the
wrong path, and she thought she should not find

the mill again, when she came out into a field,
just opposite Rocreuse. As soon as she caught
sight of the village, she stopped. Was she going
to return alone?

As she stood there, a voice called to her
softly,—

—— " Françoise ! Françoise ! "

And she saw Dominique raising his head
above the edge of a ditch. Just God! she had
found him ! So heaven wished his death? She
held back a cry, she let herself slide down into
the ditch.

—— " You were looking for me ? " he asked.

—— " Yes," she answered, her head buzzing,
not knowing what she said.

—— " Ah ! what 's going on ? "

She looked down, she stammered out,—

——" Why, nothing ; I was anxious, I wanted
to see you."

Then, reassured, he told her that he had not
wished to go far. He feared for them. Those
rascals of Prussians were just the sort to wreak
vengeance upon women and old men. Then
all was going well ; and he added, laughing,—

—— " Our wedding will be for this day week,
that 's all."

Then, as she was still overcome, he grew
serious again.

—— " But what 's the matter with you ? You
are keeping something from me."

—— " No, I swear to you. I ran to come. . . ."

He kissed her, saying that it was imprudent for either of them to talk any longer; and he wished to get back to the forest. She held him back. She was trembling.

—— " Listen, perhaps it would be as well for you to stay here, all the same. . . . Nobody is looking for you, you 're not afraid of anything."

—— " Françoise, you are keeping something from me," he repeated.

Again she swore she was keeping nothing from him. Only she had rather know that he was near; and she stammered out other reasons besides. She struck him as acting so queerly, that now he himself would not have been willing to leave her. Besides, he believed the French would return. Troops had been seen over Sauval way.

—— " Ah! let them be in a hurry, let them be here as soon as possible!" he muttered fervently.

At this moment the Rocreuse church clock struck eleven. The strokes came clear and distinct. She sprang up in fright; it was two hours since she had left the mill.

—— " Listen," she said rapidly, "if we should need you, I will go up to my room and wave my handkerchief."

And she left him, running, while Dominique, very anxious, stretched himself out on the edge of the ditch, to keep his eye on the mill. As she was just turning into Rocreuse, Françoise met an old beggar, old Bontemps, who knew the whole country. He bowed to her, he had just seen the miller in the midst of the Prussians; then, crossing himself and mumbling some dis-connected words, he went on his way.

—— "The two hours are over," said the officer when Françoise appeared.

Old Merlier was there, sitting on the bench by the well. He was still smoking. The young girl once more implored, wept, fell upon her knees. She wished to gain time. The hope of seeing the French return had grown in her, and, while bewailing her fate, she thought she heard the measured tread of an army. Oh! if they had come, if they had delivered them all!

—— "Listen, monsieur, one hour, one hour more. . . . You can surely grant me one hour!"

But the officer was still inflexible. He even ordered two men to take her in charge and lead her away, that they might proceed quietly with the old man's execution. Then a frightful con-flict went on in Françoise's heart. She could not let her father be thus murdered. No, no, she would die with Dominique first; and she was bounding toward her room, when Dominique him-self walked into the courtyard.

The officer and soldiers gave a shout of triumph. But he, as if no one but Françoise had

been there, stepped up to her quietly, a little
sternly.

—— "That was wrong," said he. " Why
did n't you bring me back with you? Old Bontemps had to tell me everything. . . . After all,
here I am."

———

V.

IT was three o'clock. Great black clouds had
slowly filled the sky, the tail of some not distant
thunderstorm. This yellow sky, these copper-
colored rags, changed the valley of Rocreuse,
so cheerful in the sunshine, to a cut-throat den,
full of suspicious shadows. The Prussian officer
had been content to have Dominique locked up,
without saying anything about what fate he had
in store for him. Ever since noon, Françoise
had been a prey to abominable anguish. She
would not leave the courtyard, in spite of her
father's urging. She was waiting for the French.
But the hours passed by, night was at hand, and
she suffered the more keenly that all this time
gained did not seem likely to change the frightful catastrophe.

Nevertheless, at about three, the Prussians
made preparations to go. A minute before, the
officer had closeted himself with Dominique, as
on the preceding day. Françoise saw that the
young man's life was being decided on. Then

she clasped her hands and prayed. Old Merlier, beside her, maintained his mute and rigid attitude of an old peasant who does not struggle with the fatality of facts.

—— "Oh, my God! oh, my God!" stammered Françoise, "they are going to kill him."

The miller drew her close to him and took her upon his knees, like a child.

Just then the officer came out, while, behind him, two men led Dominique.

—— "Never, never!" cried the latter. "I am ready to die."

—— "Think of it well," replied the officer. "This service that you refuse us will be done for us by another. I offer you your life, I am generous. . . . It is only to be our guide to Montredon, through the woods. There must be paths."

Dominique made no answer.

—— "Then you are still obstinate?"

—— "Kill me, and let us have done with it," he answered.

Françoise, with hands clasped, implored him from across the yard. She had forgotten all, she would have urged him to some piece of cowardice. But old Merlier grasped her hands, that the Prussians might not see her delirious gesture.

—— "He is right," he murmured, "it's better to die."

The firing party was there. The officer was

6

waiting for a moment of weakness on Dominique's part. He still counted on winning him over. There was a dead silence. From the distance were heard violent claps of thunder. A sultry heat weighed upon the country; and, in the midst of this silence, a shriek burst forth,—

—— "The French! the French!"

It was really they. On the Sauval road, on the outskirts of the wood, you could make out the line of red trousers. Inside the mill there was an extraordinary hubbub. The Prussian soldiers ran about with guttural exclamations. For the rest, not a shot had been fired yet.

—— "The French! the French!" screamed Françoise, clapping her hands.

She was like mad. She had broken loose from her father's embrace, and she laughed, her arms waving in the air. At last they were coming, and they had come in time, since Dominique was still there, erect!

A terrible firing that burst upon her ears like a thunder-stroke made her turn round. The officer had just muttered:

—— "First of all, let us finish this job."

And, pushing Dominique up against the wall of a shed with his own hands, he had ordered, "Fire!" When Françoise turned round, Dominique was lying on the ground, his breast pierced with twelve bullets.

She did not weep; she stood there in a stupor.

Her eyes were fixed, and she went and sat down
under the shed, a few steps from the body. She
looked at it; at moments she made a vague and
childlike movement with her hand. The Prussians had laid hold of old Merlier as a hostage.

It was a fine fight. Rapidly the officer stationed his men, recognizing that he could not
beat a retreat without being overpowered. It
was as well to sell his life dearly. Now it was
the Prussians who defended the mill and the
French that made the attack. The firing began
with unheard-of violence. For half an hour it
did not stop. Then a dull explosion was heard,
and a shot broke off one of the main branches
of the hundred-year-old elm. The French had
cannon. A battery, drawn up just above the
ditch in which Dominique had hidden, swept the
main street of Rocreuse. From this moment
the struggle could not last long.

Ah! the poor mill! Shot pierced it through
and through. Half the roofing was carried
away. Two walls crumbled. But it was, above
all, on the side toward the Morelle that the ruin
done was piteous. The ivy, torn from the shat-
tered walls, hung in rags; the river swept away
débris of every sort, and through a breach you
could see Françoise's room, with her bed, the
white curtains of which were carefully drawn.
Shot upon shot, the old wheel received two can-
non-balls, and gave one last groan: the paddles

were washed away by the current, the carcass collapsed. The mill had breathed out its soul.

Then the French stormed the place. There was a furious fight with side-arms. Beneath the rust-colored sky, the cutthroat hollow of the valley was filled with killed. The broad meadows looked grim, with their great single trees, their rows of poplars streaking them with shadows. To the right and left, the forests were like the walls of a circus, shutting in the combatants; while the springs, the fountains, the running waters, gave forth sounds of sobbing, amid the panic of the countryside.

Under the shed, Françoise had not stirred, crouched down opposite Dominique's body. Old Merlier was killed outright by a spent bullet. Then, when the Prussians had been annihilated, and the mill was burning, the French captain was the first man to enter the courtyard. From the beginning of the campaign it was the only success he had won. And, all aglow, drawing up his tall figure to its full height, he laughed with his gracious air of a fine cavalier. And, seeing Françoise, imbecile, between the dead bodies of her husband and father, amidst the smoking ruins of the mill, he gallantly saluted her with his sword, crying out:

—— "Victory! victory!"

THE VIRGIN'S GOD-CHILD

BY

EMILE SOUVESTRE

From " Tales of Brittany and La Vendee."

THE VIRGIN'S GOD-CHILD

BY EMILE SOUVESTRE

THE Bay of Douarnenez, inclosed as it is by the two rocky peninsulas of Kelerne and Crozon, which leave only a narrow passage out into the open sea, belongs to those portions of the coast of Brittany which make the deepest impression upon a traveller possessed of taste and sympathy for such scenery. Its charm does not, however, consist in what is generally called the beautiful, or the romantic. There are along this coast many wilder, sublimer, more romantic, and more beautiful points. But that which exercises so peculiar an influence here is doubtless the complete unity of style, if one may use such an expression, the harmony of the whole, and of every detail, down to the very moss which hangs from the rocks, partaking, as they all do, of one and the same grave, severe, gloomy, and mysterious character. Yet this coast-scene is preserved from a dull monotony by the exquisitely blue waters of the bay, which, though protected indeed from the mighty waves that break upon the rocky promontories outside, yet not only curls beneath the breath of the almost spent wind, and shares the great pulsations of ocean in its ebb and flow, but is still further animated by, as it were, a ceaseless breathing, or, in other words, a peculiar, mysterious, perfectly regular, and low-murmuring swelling and subsiding of its waters. Whatever explanation may be afforded by natural causes dependent upon the formation of the shore, it is certain that the people connect this phenomenon with the tradition, according to which the old Armorican King Grallon still dwells in his glorious magic city, deep down under the surface of the bay.

After a long absence I revisited this country a few years ago, to recover from the effects of the marrow and bone, the soul and spirit consuming business of the metropolis. I had wandered away to the northern tongue of land, my whole being open to the impressions conveyed by its scenery, and to the influence of the strengthening sea breeze which blew over me from both sides, to the left from the bay, to the right from the open sea. Opposite Rostudel, not far from the hamlet of Kerkolleorch, I observed, on my left, a little green dingle which opened out between gray masses of rocks, and led down to the shore of the bay. Below me, the little brook which had given rise to a kindly vegetation around—to grass, bushes, and some

low trees—had been, by the help of a few rough,
upright stones, converted into a well that a few
willows shaded over.

A young peasant girl sat on a stone near this
well, her arm resting upon one of the large red
earthern jugs which are universally used in these
parts, and have from time immemorial been
brought over from the opposite coast of Corn-
wall, which was once inhabited by a kindred
race. I stepped towards her; for even at a distance I was attracted by the peculiar and sur-
prising charm of such an apparition in this lonely
and savage spot. She was of a remarkably
pure and touching order of beauty, and the simple costume of the district, poor but delicately
clean, the blue gown with a broad red border,
the brown kerchief around the head, and which
fell over her shoulders and bosom like a pair of
wings, the small bare feet, the round arm leaning
on the red pitcher—all formed an unspeakably
charming *tout ensemble*. She greeted me in the
dialect of the country, with so gentle a voice,
and such a frank, friendly glance and nod, that
I could not resist the temptation to become
somewhat better acquainted with her, which
would, I knew, in all probability be the result of
a little conversation. As I approached, returning her greeting, and wiping away the drops that
stood on my brow, she praised the water of the
well, and offered me some to drink; and upon

my making a sign of assent, she rose, and, with fascinating grace and alacrity, raised the pitcher to my lips. While I drained long draughts of the pure stream, she held the heavy pitcher and looked at me with a smile.

As, according to the custom of the country, I thanked her by bidding God bless her, and was about to enter into conversation, a harsh voice broke in :

"The Holy Trinity protect us! Can it be Dinorah, who, on the open heath, sets up a liquor-shop for the townsfolk ?"

I looked round, and saw a miller of the neighborhood, whom I knew by sight, sitting upon his sacks, which a strong horse carried without difficulty together with his master, and on his way apparently to one hamlet after another. Under other circumstances he would have been a welcome companion to me, for he knew the country and its inhabitants intimately, and, apart from his self-satisfied, levelling, liberal views, and the spirit of contradiction which he caught from his newspapers—apart, I say, from this, and an utter absence of all feeling for what was deepest, tenderest, and most earnest in the heart of the people, he was by no means a bad sort of man, nay, for every-day life, he might be called a cheerful and useful companion.

At this moment, however, his appearance, and the antagonism between him and such a creature as Dinorah, as well as his discordance with the place, and with all that united to form the mood which he disturbed, were extremely unwelcome to me. Half offended, half embarrassed, I was silent, and turned away, that I might not be tempted to say anything rude to him. But Dinorah did not long owe him an answer.

"Go your ways elsewhere, *Guiller Three-Tongues*," cried she, with a gay and unconstrained laugh. "You are well entitled to the nickname else you never could speak so much arrant nonsense."

"Come, come, girl, give me at least a drink as well," said he conciliatingly, while he saluted me very politely—for he knew me at once, in spite of my turning away.

"Not I, indeed," replied she tartly. "This is only spring-water for good Christians; such as you want *fire-water*, and that I do not sell; so go your ways."

"My time is thine, child; for it so happens that I am taking this flour to Kerkolleorch."

"Except that portion of it which remains behind sticking to the mill-stones—is it not so, Guiller?"

I could not help laughing at this allusion to the well-known foible of the miller, or rather at the droll, pert way in which the girl brought it out; but the miller turned to me, and said, with a shrug of his shoulders:

"Monsieur, then, understands the *gour lar chenn* (the bad tongue) already. But who ever would believe it of a little saint that she could be so sharp? I have seen her when she was not higher than her pitcher—when she could not even call me by my name, and now I can get on less well with her than if she were an advocate. That shows plainly enough that when God took the tongue from the serpent He gave it to the woman. I should like to know if she serves *Bauzec the Black* in the same way when he passes by her door."

The miller had evidently touched his fair opponent on a tender point. At all events she was silent, blushed perceptibly, and pulled her head-gear about with some embarrassment. But when he tried to follow up his advantage, she soon found her tongue again, and some light-hearted and harmless bantering was carried on between them for some time longer.

At last, he replied to the reproach of not knowing how to prevent his three tongues from contradicting each other, by an allusion that I did not understand, and which soon put an end to all jesting on the part of Dinorah.

"Well," cried he, "we can't all be the blessed Virgin's god-children—*that* is only the lot of such little saints as Dinorah."

"Do not mock at holy things, Guiller," said she, with a sudden earnestness of voice, look,

and gesture, while raising her pitcher to her head,
and preparing to go away.

"Old William * may burn me black," replied
he, "if I meant to mock. Every child in the
district knows the story, and if the gentleman has
not heard it already, I will tell it him now.

"You must know that the little Dinorah was
just born, and was to be, as is right and proper,
baptized as soon as possible. All were assembled in the church, and quite ready. The sexton
had brought the shell with the salt in it—the
priest had put on his stole; they were only waiting for one of the godmothers. At that moment
came a messenger out of breath to say that she
had suddenly dropped down dead. You may
imagine the confusion and distress. It would
never do to take the first come for the godmother of such a jewel of a child, and in short
she was very near being carried out of the church
unbaptized, home. At that moment, out of the
Chapel of the Holy Virgin Mary, which stands
on one side of the choir, there came a wonderfully beautiful lady, dressed in silk and lace, and
offered to hold the child for baptism. The priest
had nothing to say against it, and all the rest of
the party assembled held their breath at the
apparition; and before they rightly knew what

* This is the title given by the peasants of Brittany to
the devil—perhaps from a forgotten play upon the name
of William the Conqueror.

had happened to them, our little Dinorah was
baptized, and the apparition had vanished again
into the chapel. But pray, sir, do not think of
disputing with Dinorah here, or with any of the
good folk of this province, as to whether it really
was the Blessed Virgin, or a distinguished lady
'from Paris, who was sketching at that time in the
neighborhood, and hunting out cromlechs and
other antiquities and curiosities. So now you see
it was no bad joke of mine, but that it is in good,
downright earnest that we call Dinorah the little
saint, and the Virgin's god-daughter!"

I looked inquiringly at Dinorah, who replied,
half in anger and half in embarrassment :

" Guiller can lie, even while telling the truth ;
but, however, no one can alter what God willed
should happen. The dog may bark at the moon,
indeed ; but the moon does not, on that account,
fall from the sky."

So saying, she went away with a quick step,
and soon disappeared behind the rocks.

We took the same way more slowly. The miller went on rattling for some time, but I did not
heed him. The little legend I had just heard
had in no way diminished my interest in Dinorah.
I knew well that the people in Brittany are always
pleased with stories of some wonderful distinction
paid to one or other of themselves by the Lord of
Heaven, or by some of His saints. Such highly
favored ones are objects of pride to a whole

district. I had already heard of the widow of a baker of St. Mathieu, whose dough had been kneaded by the archangel Gabriel; and of Lotsen of Batz, to whom the Saviour Himself had taught certain words which had the power of guiding a ship safely over the most perilous seas, and had never yet seen one of these distinguished individuals. Here, however, was a maiden who was evidently fully persuaded that she stood in a peculiar relation to the Queen of Heaven. No one who saw her could doubt the genuineness of such belief on her part; nay, this story alone gave the key to her peculiar bearing—at once lively and dignified, modest, retiring, mysterious, and yet firm, self-possessed, and even daring as it was. Moreover—as Guiller confessed cordially enough, when he found that his light talk found no response in me—though Dinorah was certainly rather too proud of her exalted sponsor, she did her credit by being the most pious, most honorable, and, in short, the best girl in all the country far and near; and if all saints were like her, added he, he would himself think seriously about being converted and trying to get to heaven.

Meanwhile, we had reached one of those cottages standing close by the shore, where the so-called *Gabariers* were wont to live, that they might collect tang, fine sand, and other productions or refuse of the sea, which they sold to potash and glass manufacturers, in order to eke

out by these small earnings the fishing which was
their special vocation.   But this cottage of which
I speak was in far better order than the general-
ity.   It was built of granite blocks, pretty regularly arranged, and roofed with large slates.   Its
situation was sheltered, standing as it did at the
opening of a little hollow in the steep banks which
rose from behind it, leaving room for a little bit
of garden, where herbs and a few flowers, protected by a green hedge, seemed to flourish very
well.   A deep curve of the shore reached to a few
steps of the cottage door.   The little waves,
sparkling in the evening sun, lifted in their play
a neat boat on to the snow-white sand of the
beach, which was diversified here and there by
gay shells.   Nets were hanging up to dry upon a
neighboring rock.

Guiller observed to me :

" That's the home of Dinorah's father, old Salaun.   And there lies the old man himself," con-'
tinued he, laughing, as he pointed out a man
asleep in the shadow of a rock, " and repeats the
paternoster of St. Do-nothing.   These people
live as they used to do in Paradise.   The sea
brings them all they want while they sleep, and
they have only got to stretch their hand out to
take it in.   No doubt he is dreaming at this moment of the great lobster with pearl eyes, and of
the bank with silver anchovies ; and he is ready
to sell his soul to Satan if he will but get him a

net made of sand, with which to fish out all these marvels from the depths of the Bay of Douarnenez. I will waken him just in time to prevent the bargain being struck."

He did this in rather a summary manner; and after a few jokes, both men began to unlade the sacks of flour which the miller had brought. During this process I engaged the Gabarier to take me in his boat, at the next ebb of the tide, to the cave of Morgate, which was opposite, at the very extremity of the southern point. To while away the short intervening time, I ascended the banks behind the cottage, and delighted myself with the glorious scene presented by the bay: its rocky shores, the wide sea beyond, the promontories and fissures far and near, the hundred sails of small and large vessels traversing the blue expanse in every direction; and all this brightly lighted up by the sun, which already neared the misty horizon.

I was roused out of the dreamy condition into which the scene had plunged me by the noise that the fisherman and miller made in shutting the cottage-door after they had finished their task. I had begun to descend, but involuntarily stood still as I saw Dinorah come out of the cottage. She had placed her distaff on her hip, and as she went along she whirled the spindle with great speed and accuracy. In the other hand, she held up her apron, in which she seemed

7

to be carrying something or other. She came up
the cliff near to where I was standing, behind a
projection of rock, and then stood still, a few
steps below me. She looked round on every side,
raised her hand to the four points of the compass
successively, while she pronounced two or three
words which I did not understand. She was instantly answered by a loud chirping from the low
bushes around, and from every side different
kinds of birds—bulfinches, robin-redbreasts,
hedge-sparrows, titmice, and many more—flew
down to pick up the food she had brought them
in her apron, and which she now carefully and
lovingly distributed in little handfuls, while, in
an undertone, she sang to herself in a strange
sort of way.

It was a lovely picture, seen thus in the red
glow of evening; and the pure outline of her face,
with its rich waves of golden hair around, would
certainly have afforded to a painter a most admirable study for the head of a saint.

At length I approached, but she beckoned me
away, without, however, evincing the least surprise or embarrassment.

"If monsieur comes nearer, all my little birdies
will fly away, and they are not half satisfied,"
said she in a whisper, that her *protégés* might not
be disturbed by the sound of a strange language.

However, at that moment both the men came
noisily out of the cottage, and the little birds dis-

persed on every side, with a loud twittering, expressive of their alarm and displeasure.

So Dinorah, after having called out a few quieting and sympathizing words after them, found herself obliged to speak to me. In answer to my question, by what means she had contrived thus to tame such shy little creatures, she looked at me in astonishment, and said:

"Why, by the same that attracts all God's creatures—by love; by showing them that one is fond of them. In winter, when they cannot find food for themselves, I strew it for them before our door, and in summer they know me again."

As she spoke, we reached the cottage, and the miller could not refrain from teasing her a little more.

"The little saint has again given alms to the beggars of the air. No doubt she expects to find one or other amongst them who will bring her tidings from her high and holy godmother."

Dinorah went into the house, silent, and evidently offended; but old Salaun said gravely:

"And why not, pray? If our fathers have not deceived us, there are birds who know the way to the *upper sea*, and can, no doubt, carry a message to the blest in Paradise."

"Well, all I know," replied the miller, "is that it is just the contrary with my horse and me. We have to find our way to one who comes much

nearer to the lost in hell.   Or has the devil at last
hunted down his prey—*Judock Shipwreck* of the
Ravens' Cliff?"

Salaun, it was plain, wished to avoid giving an
answer, and went accordingly towards the boat,
remarking that it was high time to think of our
expedition.   But the name of *Judock* happened
to recall to my mind, though indistinctly, certain
criminal prosecutions in which I had been engaged.   And upon inquiry the miller convinced
me that it was indeed this very man who had
been brought before the Court at Brest several
years before, charged with heavy crimes, but who
had been acquitted, contrary to the general expectation, owing to some deficiency in the evi-
dence.

"If I only knew," added the miller, "whether
the old villain were at home, that he might himself receive his flour from me, and make no more
ado about it, I would rather"—here he interrupted himself.   "But here comes his boy—
Bauzec the Black—and he can give us the surest
information if he but choose to do so."

The new-comer was a young lad in the very
poorest dress of the district.   His thick, unkempt,
rough, coal-black hair fell like a mane over his
shoulders.   In his right hand he held a long
cudgel, which, with strength and agility, he swung
round in circles; while his left hand clutched
with fierce grasp the sack which he carried on

his shoulders. His features, as well as his expression, wore no trace of the old Armorican type, had about them nothing of its sad, severe earnestness and indomitable fidelity. There was evidently the wild, cunning, gypsy character about the dark, contracted features, and the bright, deeply cut eyes. In short, there was something in his whole appearance that awakened dislike as well as fear.

When he saw that he was observed, he stopped for an instant in his rapid walk, and seemed doubtful as to whether or not he would turn back. But just at that moment Dinorah happened to come to the door, busied with her spindle, and looking down.

As soon as he saw her, he came on again, but so slowly, that the miller more than once called upon him to make haste, adding, that in general he was light-footed enough, otherwise there would have been an end of his light feet long ago, and he would have had a couple of pounds of iron hung upon them. When the lad had come within a few steps of us, he stood still again, and cast furtive glances—differing, however, wonderfully in expression—first at us, and then at Dinorah. The miller then asked him if Judock was at home. He made no answer till Dinorah repeated the question, when he slowly said :

"He only can know that who comes from the Ravens' Cliff."

"And thou, lad, comest as usual," said the fisherman, advancing towards us from his boat, "only from some place or other thou shouldest not come from, and which no one asks thee about."

"Where should he come from, indeed, but from some poaching expedition?" suggested the miller. "Let us see what your booty is to-day—fruit or roots, fish or flesh!"

And so saying, he was going to snatch at the sack, but the youth looked at him in such a way, and made such an expressive motion with the cudgel, that the miller, strong as he was, drew back, with an exclamation that called forth the interposition of Dinorah.

"Bauzec comes from the downs," she calmly said; "I saw him wandering about there an hour or so ago."

"He has been hunting with the gentry. I have met him out with them before now," exclaimed Guiller spitefully.

"And why not?" replied the youth, in a tone of defiance. "Here is my gun, which never fails, and here is my sporting dog, which never loses scent of the game," added he triumphantly, as he swung round his cudgel, and opened his sack a little, out of which peeped a little white, hairy head, with small, red eyes, and a pointed and blood-stained little nose.

"A ferret!" exclaimed Salaun; "no wonder,

then. that the gentry complain that they can hardly get a roasted rabbit out of all their rabbit-warrens."

Bauzec grinned with delight at this acknowledgment of his heroic deeds. He fumbled in his bag, and brought out four fine rabbits, on whose white breasts the little track of blood showed where the ferret had sucked their veins. That little creature evinced a strong fellow-feeling with his master, looking complacently upon its victims, and licking its lips and whiskers with its small red tongue.

To the miller's question as to whether he was willing to sell them, Bauzec replied:

"Not here; I shall get a better price for them at the tavern in Crozon, as well as a glass of fire-water into the bargain."

So saying, he replaced his booty in the bag, lingered for a moment or two as if in indecision, and then prepared. to leave without any further salutation. But he suddenly recollected himself, drew one of the rabbits out of the bag again, and threw it at Dinorah's feet, with the bold yet shy manner of a rough youth who would willingly be gallant but does not know how.

"It is the finest of them," muttered he; "the little saint may keep it if she will."

Dinorah looked at him gravely, almost severely. But her father pushed away the present with his foot, and said rudely: "Take thy game along with thee, lad; we only receive presents from Christian people."

Bauzec shrank back, and for a moment appeared discomfited; but he soon regained his savage air of defiance. He uttered a sort of hissing sound, which might pass for a laugh of contempt, took up his bag again, and with a few strides vanished behind a projection of the rocks.

The miller, meanwhile, had picked up the rabbit, and said that his conscience was not so tender; and that, if they despised the dainty roast it would make, it would do nicely for him.

He then prepared to join Bauzec, as he had to go to the Ravens' Cliff. I resolved to accompany him; for I was curious to make the personal acquaintance of this Judock, whose innocence as to the charges already referred to had always appeared to me something more than doubtful, while their nature had left on my mind a picture of a remarkable and original villain. The fisherman promised, though evidently with some reluctance, to bring the boat round for me to Ravens' Cliff at the proper time. I took a short farewell of Dinorah, but found her far more silent and reserved than she had been at first, and went on my way, accompanied by the miller.

"You will find Judock an odd sort of saint," said my companion, in his obtrusive way; "or rather, I should say, no saint at all, but a regular limb of Satan, with whose sins and crimes one could fill up the whole way between Camaret and Crozon. For twenty years he lit false lights from Loquirnk to Trevignon, and has had more to do with shipwrecks upon this coast than the south-west wind itself."

I asked whether this creditable occupation enriched its pursuer.

"One cannot exactly tell," rejoined Guiller; "he lives in his den yonder as poor as a *Klasker-bara*—a bread-seeker, as we call beggars about here. But the question is, whether his miserliness be not greater than all his other vices. Many believe that he has tons of buried gold. And besides, he gains something every now and then as a flayer and rope-maker; and on that account, too, the people look askance at him as anything but a Christian, and aver that he is a Kakous."

After an hour's good walk, as we followed a bend of the down, we came in sight of Judock's hut. It was built into a small and narrow fissure in the rocks, and stood close to the shore. The natural walls thus afforded, the moss-grown flagstones that formed its roof, and whose broad crevices were stuffed up with sea-tang, held together by strong fir-branches, rendered it difficult to distinguish the dwelling from the rocks around, and the sea-produce strewn upon them.

Everything was barren, rude, and inhospitable-looking. Some pointed piles of bones lay about, and the projecting roof of the gable had two or three horses' skulls nailed to it, a decoration worthy of the whole.

Judock sat at his door, busied with some old cordage, which he was pulling to pieces. He was a little, thin, shrivelled old man, with a large bald head. The prevailing hue of his face was almost brick-colored, but in the countless wrinkles the skin was lighter; and as these wrinkles widened more or less at every change of feature, or when he spoke, they gave him a strange repulsive appearance, and made a varying and confusing impression upon the beholder. His restless, piercing glance, his beak-like nose, his low forehead, his toothless mouth, his under jaw in constant motion,—all completed a picture which only answered too well to the opinion that I had already formed of him.

As soon as he saw me he started, and furtively watched all my movements with visible unrest and suspicion. But he pretended not to observe me.

"Now then, old sinner," said Guiller to him at last, "canst thou not give God's blessing and the good-day to this gentleman?"

"What is the nobleman seeking for on this coast?" was the ungracious answer, spoken in an undertone.

"Ay, what indeed?—old Judock, perhaps," said the miller, laughing.

At these words Judock sprang up, and seemed doubtful whether to flee or to defend himself. I however soon calmed him, by assuring him that I was only a lover of rock and ocean, and that I had a boat ready to take me to see the cave. Without returning me any answer, he seized the sack of flour that Guiller had brought, and carried it into the hut. No sooner had I crossed the threshold, however, than Judock let his burden fall and gave a loud scream.

"He here!" exclaimed he, with an expression of extremest amazement. "The saints be gracious to me! how has *he* got in?"

The intruder was Bauzec, who, to all appearance quite unconcerned, sat upon the hearth and roasted potatoes in the ashes.

"Why," observed the miller, showing himself upon the doorsill, "you have not left more than one hole to your palace; how could he have got in otherwise than by it, old boy?"

"No, no; the door was shut, and I—but I must ferret out how this vermin crept in here without my knowledge, or—"

He raised his hand threateningly against the lad, who, however, replied calmly, and with an ironical emphasis upon the expression:

"Why, my *dear father*, does not the wind find its way in without asking your leave, and why should not your dear little son do the same?"

"Only hear him, the young imp!" exclaimed the old man, half angrily and half piteously. "He himself confesses that he has slipped in here to rob his poor old father!"

"Eh, father dear!" continued the youth in the same mocking tone; "so there is then something to rob you of, and people are not so far wrong—eh?"

That last sentence was too much for the old man. He seized an iron implement which lay at hand, and rushed upon Bauzec; but with a laugh he slipped away from him, and out at the door, with cat-like agility. The old man followed, but he very soon returned out of breath, apparently without having effected anything. He spent himself in asseverations respecting his poverty, his age, and his wretchedness; the untruth, and indeed impossibility, of any reports to the contrary; the bad-heartedness and ingratitude of the "vermin," as he called his well-educated son.

The miller put an end to the repulsive garrulity of the old man—whose mind was actually weakened by the alarm given to his covetousness—by reminding him of the payment due, and of the glass of brandy that was to accompany it. But he could only bring him to the point by the positive threat of no longer grinding for him.

At last the boat of old Salaun touched the

shore, and he called out to me that there was no time to lose. I was glad to leave the inhospitable hut and its owner, and the miller too, whose manner towards the old man was disagreeable to me. So I soon found myself sitting in the boat, and gave myself up to the strange and sublime scenes that shore and sea afforded me, as he rowed to the outlet of the bay. Salaun had made visible haste to push off from the shore, and had at first exerted all his energies to get away as fast as possible out of sight of the Kakous' hut.

His exertions, and the anxious look that he cast towards the cloudless horizon, induced me at last to ask him whether we had a sudden squall to apprehend.

"Ask them who cause such, sir; it would not be the first storm that has come from that quarter in perfectly still weather," said he significantly, while he pointed to the direction where stood the dwelling of the Kakous.

And strange enough, at that very moment, a light white cloud arose from the point in question, and spread out to the horizon. But I soon convinced myself that it must be smoke and concerned myself no further about the matter, seeing that the Gabarier, to my query as to how a fire could take place on so nearly uninhabited a coast, merely replied by shrugs of the shoulders and other strange gestures. And besides this, we had now reached the vicinity of the Grotto of Morgate, where Nature claimed and absorbed all my attention.

I let the conversation drop, and soon we glided through the narrow entrance into the cave, whose noble dome—looking, in the wonderfully blue light, as if it were built of sapphires—rose suddenly upon the astonished and bewildered sight. This cave certainly surpasses the so much more widely famed blue Grotto of Capri; and this particular point, as well as the whole coast indeed, possesses, in a much higher degree than those southern shores, the charm of ancient local traditions and national songs.

These are for the most part connected, in this district, with the mythic King Grallon-Mawr (Grallon the Great), and with the magic Princess Morgane, or Morgate, who, as is well known, occupies so prominent a position in the legends and lays of Arthur's Round Table.

Nothing was wanting but a hint on my part to induce my companion, who had been hitherto so monosyllabic, to set off fluently upon these subjects.

His favorite tradition—the scene of which, moreover, was, he asserted, this very grotto— appeared to be the story of the fair Genossa, which is also preserved in an old national song (*Guerz*) of Brittany.*

---

* It is well known that the distinguished Villemarque has published a collection, in two volumes, of similar

Genossa was the daughter of a mighty lord, who lived in the castle whose giant ruins are still shown on the island of Rozan, at the mouth of the Laber. Genossa lived without God, and without a wish. Her father let her grow up as do the flowers of the field, and no priest had ever approached the island, which was devoted to the Evil Spirit. Sitting upon a snow-white cow with golden horns, she wandered all the day long through the meadows and woods that lay around the shore, catching in her silken net the birds on the wing.

One day she chanced to meet a beautiful young man upon a black bull with silver horns. His approach thrilled her through and through. He spoke such wondrously sweet words to her, that she was bewitched by them. The black bull and the white cow walked so closely together, and so slowly, that they could crop the grass at their feet, and pull at the same flowers; and the blended sound of their hoofs echoed like music in the heart of Genossa.

The fisherman had at first told the tale in his own way, and with sundry pauses; but soon the words of the old ditty fell from him in their original form, and he continued without interrup-

national lyrics, under the title, *Barzas-Briez, chants populaires de la Brétagne*, which have also been translated by Ad. Keller, and others whose names have escaped my memory. But the legend of Genossa is not amongst them.

tion, in a strange half-chanting, half-reciting tone :

"It seemed to Genossa as though every tree were hung around with wreaths of flowers, and sweet bird-notes sprung from under every leaf, and the sea breezes were laden with incense-like perfume. Genossa met the handsome man on the black bull more than once, and ever his magic power grew stronger and stronger over her. She soon thought and wished only what the stranger wished and thought. And so it came to pass that one day the white cow returned to the castle alone, and Genossa sat behind the stranger upon the black bull with the silver horns. The lord of the island of Rozan, however, gathered all his men together in pursuit, each bearing in one hand a sword, and in the other a dagger. For this lord had promised to cover with gold every drop of blood spilt, whether of their own or their enemy's.

"Soon Genossa found herself resting by the stranger's side on the sea-shore, while the black bull pastured near. As soon as the stranger saw the pursuers advancing, he vaulted with Genossa on the back of the bull, who plunged into the blue sea, and soon carried them over to the Grotto of Morgane. Arrived there, the stranger began to caress the maiden; she shrank away abashed, and said :

"'Leave off, Spountus.* I hear my mother weeping and sobbing between the boards of the narrow house.'

"'It is the sighing of the waves in the narrow fissures of the rock, my sweet Genossa.'

"'Listen, listen, Spountus! my mother speaks from under the consecrated earth!'

"'What says she, then, from under the consecrated earth, Genossa?'

"'She says that her daughter is not to give herself up body and soul without the show of consecrated altar-lights, and without the priest's holy chants.'

"'Be it, then, as she wishes, Genossa, my beloved; I honor the dead!'

"Then the handsome stranger made a sign, and suddenly there rose out of the darkness priest and choristers, and surrounded the rock that rises in the little island in the midst of the grotto. They covered the rock with a cloth of scarlet silk embroidered in silver, and kindled around it tall wax lights in golden candlesticks. The marriage ceremony began. But at the moment when the priest spoke the blessing, and placed the ring upon her finger, Genossa screamed aloud till the whole grotto rang with the sound. The ring burned her finger like fire. She tried to tear herself away—to fly, but it was

* *Spountus*, the Terrible, is one of the names given to the Evil Spirit by the Armorican Celts.

8

too late ! Spountus seized her arm, and forced her to follow him through long, endlessly long and dismal passages. Her heart died within her, and, trembling and sorrowful, she leaned on the one who had become master of her soul and body.

"'Listen, Spountus,' whispered she, 'does it not seem as if all around us—here, there, and everywhere—there came the sounds of weeping and wailing and gnashing of teeth?'

"'It is nothing, Genossa, my sweet soul, but the workmen who are boring the rock above us, and singing their songs the while.'

"'Seems it not, Spountus, as though bitter tears were trickling on us down the rocks?'

"'It is only the water of the springs that oozes through the rock, Genossa, my sweet soul.'

"'Lord of my life, the air that surrounds us is like the breath of a furnace!'

"'Genossa, joy of my heart, look there! Fire, fire, everywhere fire! this is hell, heathen maiden, and thou art mine for ever!'"

This is the *Guerz* of Genossa, which must of course lose indescribably by translation, and by the absence of all the circumstances under which I heard it.

We rowed once more in silence round the devil's altar, and by way of dispelling the oppressive and shuddering mood into which the old song had unconsciously plunged me, I inquired whether Spountus were still occasionally to be seen in the grotto. The fisherman did not answer at once, but first with a couple of powerful oar-strokes made the boat shoot out through the entrance of the grotto into the clear daylight and the free expanse of sea. Then he said:

"The gentleman ought to have asked old Judock that question—he knows its answer."

As it was evident that my companion had no pleasure in telling either what he knew or what he thought upon this subject, and as moreover we were suddenly surrounded by a thick fog, occasioning all manner of optical illusions, and requiring his whole attention to be given to the management of the boat, we both continued silent. But after about a quarter of an hour, when a fresh wind rose and drove away the fog, Salaun suddenly touched me on the shoulder, exclaiming:

"Look there! Judock's hut is on fire!"

On looking round, I remarked a ruddy light on the Ravens' Cliff, which was scarcely distinguished from the rosy glow still thrown by the setting sun upon the higher rocks. It was only at intervals that a brighter flame leaped up. Agreeably to my wish, Salaun steered our boat to the spot; curiosity, or the wish to assist, overcoming the repugnance which he had previously shown to the Ravens' Cliff and to its owner.

As we drew near we saw a number of men

busily engaged about the fire, while numbers
more were hurrying towards it in every direction.
Having landed, we soon found out that, as is
generally the case on such occasions, the greatest part of them by screams and useless gestures
impeded the assistance that might yet have been
afforded. A few only were occupied with the
door, which, however, they had vainly tried to
break open with the half of a fir-tree stem torn
off the roof, while the fire appeared to be de-
vouring slowly the inside of the hut, which had
no vent or opening of any kind. On approaching nearer, a loud groaning and whining was distinctly heard within. We listened for a moment;
another voice arose, a sharp, mocking tone,
which at last broke out into a yell of fiendish
laughter. Then hard blows were repeatedly
given—then again the same wailing and whim-
pering, the same mocking rejoinder.

Salaun and the remainder drew back in horror, and a few words, spoken half aloud, showed
that they were in no doubt as to whom the old
villain had to deal with, and that, in their
opinion, no human help could avail to deliver
him from the grasp of the spirits whom he had
served all his life long.

It was in vain that I requested Salaun to join
me in an attempt to break open the door.

"This fire is not kindled by mortal hands, and
we poor sinners can never put it out."

" The Church will put it out, then," here interfered a deep, well-toned voice.

It was that of a priest who had joined us. All surrounded him, taking off their hats with much respect, while I in a few words explained the state of things. Though advanced in years, he was still strong and active in mind and body. We understood each other instantly. While he sent a messenger to fetch an axe from the nearest village, and gave some other judicious orders, which the people unhesitatingly obeyed, I climbed to the top of the rock into whose fissures the hut was squeezed, that I might thence try to find out whether it had any other opening or not.

I was, however, unable to discover anything of the kind, and was therefore about to descend, when I saw a dark figure glide behind some low bushes at a little distance, but the very same moment it vanished behind the next projection of rock. It had already become too dark, and the apparition was too sudden and momentary for me to have any distinct impression as to its form or features.

At first I felt half inclined to pursue it, but after two or three onward steps I felt convinced that to do so along such a road as this, over such masses of rocks, such crevices, and through such brushwood, would be not only vain, but dangerous. At the same time, too, the strokes of the axe upon the door announced that the chief

point—that of forcing an entrance into the hut
—would soon be gained, and I therefore rapidly
made my way down again.

Just as I arrived the door gave way. A stream
of flame, clouds of smoke, and sparks rushed
out, and scared the bystanders away; but the
fury of the fire was already spent, and in a few
moments the priest was able to enter, followed
by Salaun and myself. The others remained
standing outside, partly out of respect to the in-
junctions of the priest, partly through terror of
the things that might have to be encountered
within.

The first sight that met our eyes was Judock
lying upon the hearth in a pool of blood. He
was still alive, and we instantly carried him out
into the open air; and at the earnest entreaty of
the priest, the barber of the neighboring village,
who, like the many others, found himself on the
spot, undertook to examine, and, as far as he was
able, to treat the severely-wounded man. At the
same time, all that could be done was done to
save the hut. It was found that all that was
combustible was already consumed, and the glow-
ing embers were easily quenched. No trace was
found of the perpetrator, or of the cause of the
crime, except, indeed, a mattock, which had evidently served to raise the hearthstone, and to dig
under it.

That this calamity was not accidental, we none

of us had any doubt ; and as I, in company with
the priest, again approached the late possessor
of the hut, the surgeon, as he called himself,
showed us a deep wound in the breast, and a
considerable dint in the head of the old Kakous,
which could only have been dealt by a murderer's
hand.

It was quite plain that no recovery was to be
looked for. Before we found the old man, he
had bled almost to death, and seemed to have
already entirely lost consciousness. But after a
few minutes, he came to himself a little, moved
his lips, opened his eyes, and tried, with the convulsive energy of a dying effort, to shape his loud
groans into intelligible words. If his appearance
had been repulsive in life, it was now almost in-
sufferably horrible. At length he was able to
make it understood that he wished to confess.
The bystanders seemed to look upon such a re-
quest not only with wonder, but displeasure, as
involving unheard-of presumption, and actual
desecration of the rite. But the priest knelt
down at once by the head of the dying man, and
at a sign from him the people reverentially re-
tired, the greatest part evincing their sympathy
with the solemn occasion by kneeling also, with
heads uncovered, and hands folded in silent
prayer.

The moon had by this time risen, and spread
a mild, peaceful light on the shore, the rocks, and

the sea, whose low murmur the solemn stillness
of the men, so loud a few minutes before, rendered more impressive. The silence was only
broken every now and then by the increasingly
painful groans of the dying man, or by an outburst of sparks, as some remnants of the wood-
work within the hut, or rather the cleft that it
formerly occupied, fell in.

After a few minutes, the priest beckoned me
to approach. He had, according to his appre-
hension of the duties of his calling, endeavored,
before all things, to awaken the feeble consciousness of the expiring sinner to the necessity of
preparing for death after the manner of the
Catholic Church, as far as it was possible to do
so under such circumstances. But when this
was over, he was anxious to make an attempt to
elicit some words which might lead to the discovery of the murderer; and it was with this
view that he wished to have me both as assistant
and witness—and also called old Salaun.

The dying man's words were for the most part
incoherent, and spoken in an unintelligible voice;
but, however, such as they were, they tended to
confirm a suspicion that had already crossed my
mind, and led me to connect the mysterious presence in the hut, of the youth called Bauzec, on
the occasion of my first visit, with the apparition
I had just witnessed on the rocks above. In the
mind of the dying man, shaken as it was by the

death-struggle, and the terrors of conscience, the same opinion evidently often obtained respecting the personality of his murderer, which the people are wont to offer in connection with the most varied circumstances, namely, that the Evil One had surprised him counting his ill-won wealth, and asserted his own claim to it.

But every now and then the recollection of the true state of the case would pierce through, as he repeated:

"The vermin! the black! the vermin!" over and over again, with such rage and abhorrence, that his energies seemed more and more exhausted by each repetition of the words, and at last he died in pronouncing them.

It was to me a very significant fact that Judock should, in his wanderings, use many common English phrases, which rendered it beyond a doubt that he had carried on treasonable communications with the enemy during the war, and it was with these that the criminal prosecutions already referred to were connected.

The priest and Salaun shared my conviction. But when I exclaimed with horror:

"The son the murderer of the father!" the fisherman rejoined:

"It is bad enough as it is, but Bauzec the Black is not the son of Judock Shipwreck. I myself saw him draw the fellow with his hook out of the hen-coop of a ship that had gone to pieces.

He knew best what wind had driven it upon the Ravens' Cliff. And then the little black imp sat upon the coop, and was scarcely on shore before he shook off the water like a poodle, and danced and screamed, so that it was awful to see him. But as he had been almost drowned, the country people called him 'Bauzec,' which means in the gentleman's language 'the drowned one.' "

"Judock, then, adopted him as a son?" asked I. "That is more than I should have believed of him."

"That was not the case either," replied Salaun, "but just the contrary. The boy hung upon the old man like a chain; hooked himself to him like a kitten. He could neither be shaken off nor driven away by blows, kicks, or hunger—he always returned. If Judock had flung him out at night, and driven him far away across the downs, believing that he would not find his way back; when morning came, there he was again cowering at the door. But you are not to suppose that gratitude or attachment had anything to do with this. On the contrary, from the very first he took to playing all manner of tricks upon the old man; and if he ever failed to get out of the way of blows with cat-like expertness, and chanced to be caught, which was rare, he would bite and scratch like a young wild beast. It really seemed as though he were an evil spirit, and had a hold over the old sinner's soul. At all

events, he was obliged to tolerate what he could
not avoid. For, you see, he was grown old and
feeble, and had, besides, a horror of the lad, whom
he never called by any other name than the
'vermin'; or else what could have prevented
him from tying a stone about his neck and throwing him into the sea? Certainly it was not conscience or tender-heartedness, for—"

Here Salaun interrupted himself.

"The Kakous is now dead, and has to give an
account of himself elsewhere, and so I will say
no more about him. We poor folk about here
have never doubted that Bauzec was given to
Judock Shipwreck as a plague and a punishment
—whether man or devil, it's all one."

Meanwhile the corpse had been carried into
the burnt-out hut, and a watch over it appointed
for the night. We at length contrived, by the
light of the tapers brought, to discover a narrow
opening at the end of the fissure, which wound
up to the top of the cliff, and opened out amidst
the brushwood there. This might possibly have
afforded an inlet to a slender and active youth.
But how it happened that the builder and owner
of the hut should not have been aware of this
way of entrance, or how, on the other hand, he
should not have stopped it up, fearing that his
good-for-nothing comrade might learn to make
use of it without his leave, and probably to his
hurt, this certainly did remain a mystery to us.

Midnight was already past before the country
people dispersed, and I again took my place in
the boat, to be rowed by the old fisherman to his
own dwelling. We were both silent, meditating,
no doubt, upon what we had just witnessed. We
now approached the little bay in which Salaun's
cottage stood, and by the unsteady and changing
light of the clouded moon were already able to
distinguish it, when we heard a loud cry for help
proceeding thence. The next moment two figures rushed out on the shore, and struggled vio-
lently—or rather, one struggled to overpower the
other, who endeavored to escape, and cried more
and more loudly for help.

"God be with me!" exclaimed Salaun at the
first scream heard, "it is Dinorah's voice!"

And, straining his strength to the utmost, he
made the little boat bound to the point where we
saw the two forms, while we both announced the
approach of help, and endeavored to frighten
away the assailant by raising our voices to their
utmost pitch. But, owing to the murmurs of the
waves upon the beach, and to the excitement of
the parties concerned, they did not observe us
till we were but a few yards from the shore, when
we plainly distinguished not only Dinorah, but
also the aggressor, who was no other than Bauzec
the Black. We further observed that the young
girl's strength was nearly exhausted. Dinorah
was the first to perceive us. At once she tore

herself out of her assailant's grasp, and rushed towards us into the sea.

Her father had hardly time to check the boat's speed, so as to prevent a collision, when, breathless, exhausted, with torn garment and streaming hair, she clasped the boat's prow, and was lifted into it and carried to shore in an unconscious state. Meanwhile Bauzec had vanished; and it would have been in vain to have pursued him, had we not, besides, been fully occupied with the poor girl.

Thanks to her thoroughly healthy nature, she soon came round, and told us—but not without a certain reserve, and an evident endeavor to criminate the ruffian as little as possible—that Bauzec had, about half an hour before, in great haste and excitement, joined her on the shore, whither she had gone to look for us. He had told her, in the strangest and wildest way possible, that he must leave the country forthwith, and that she must accompany him. Upon her refusal, he at first tried every means of persuasion, and showed her his hands full of gold. But when she remained firm, and again hastened out of the cottage, whither he had followed her, and rushed to the shore, he tried to carry her away by force.

"And then I cried once more out of my inmost soul to my heavenly godmother, and you came, father!" said the girl in conclusion. And the joy that beamed over her features at the miraculous help which she fully believed to have been afforded her, banished every trace of her previous terror.

Soon, however, on learning from us what had happened at the Ravens' Cliff, and recognizing, as we did also, in her late experience a confirmation of the blood-guiltiness of her wild lover, she was seized with a profound and peculiar emotion. She became pale as death, trembling in every limb, and threw herself upon her knees, where she long remained in fervent prayer.

Could the miller, Guiller, have had some grounds, then, for rallying her about this wild, repulsive, wicked youth? What relations could there possibly be between him and this pure and maidenly creature? A few words, however, exchanged upon a later occasion with the priest whose acquaintance I had made at Ravens' Cliff, afforded me the only explanation conceivable. Her feeling was a complex one, consisting in part of womanly compassion for one whom all the world, and perhaps with good cause, avoided ; in part, of a certain dread of the youth's savage strength, not entirely free, it might be, from a germ of unconscious admiration of it; in part, of blended piety and vanity, such as one often meets with in more refined society. She had believed herself elected, by the assistance and to the glory of her heavenly sponsor, to convert this poor, benighted soul.

And upon Bauzec's part, joined to the impulse of passions early wakened, there was doubtless a better and deeper impression made by the maidenly gentleness and purity of Dinorah. Wild and scornful as he was to all besides, and in outward appearance to her also, it is certain that she had obtained a degree of influence over him, which she, in her half-childish way, took pleasure in displaying.

All this, as I have already said, I only found out later. At the period of which I treat, I contented myself with leaving the father and daughter together, and betaking myself to rest in the fragrant hayloft under the roof, which was the room assigned to me.

When I awoke the following morning, the sun was already high in the heavens; nothing seemed stirring in the house, or round about it. I only heard the monotonous breaking of the waves upon the shore, and the twittering of birds between. I found the little room below in the best order possible, and even my clean and simple breakfast ready provided; but Salaun and his daughter were nowhere to be seen.

I knew too well the rights with which the inhabitants of Brittany invest the stranger—whom they designate as the *sent of God*—not to avail myself, even in the absence of the host, of the hospitality of which I stood so sorely in need. But before setting out, I laid down a gold-piece upon the table, which I could hardly have got old Salaun to accept had he been at home.

I took the way to Crozon, and had not proceeded far before I heard in the distance a solemn chant, which drew nearer and nearer to where I was. On account of the very high hedges which shut in the road, I was unable as yet to see any of the singers, even though I could distinctly hear the words of their song. A peasant who came from Crozon informed me, however, that it was a procession, undertaken by all the adjacent parishes on account of the long-continued drought, and that it was marching around the fields, chanting, and offering up prayers for rain.

From a little hillock on the roadside which I ascended, I succeeded in seeing the procession, which soon, however, defiled along a crossway, and came into the road. First came the priest, then the men, two and two; afterwards the women, in their picturesque Sunday costume, but with grave bearing, and absorbed in deep devotion.

In the pauses of the chant, which were devoted to prayer, nothing was to be heard but the humming of insects and the chirping of birds.

One of these pauses was suddenly interrupted by a noise which proceeded from the direction in which I had come. It was made by the rolling and rattling of a vehicle of some kind; and soon we could see in the lane behind us a cart, surrounded by armed custom-house officers, as well as by some fishers and peasants. The procession drew to one side to let them pass.

As the cart approached, we observed that three men were sitting upon the same seat, and that the one in the middle was chained, the other two evidently guarding him. Soon the name "Bauzec the Black," which, spoken low, went from one to the other throughout the procession, left no doubt upon my mind that it was the murderer on his way to prison. Indeed he himself took good care to give me every opportunity of recognizing him; for scarcely had the cart come up with the procession, than he raised himself from the stooping attitude he had before maintained, looked around him with the greatest audacity, and called out, to such as he was acquainted with, words of jesting or abuse, so that the good people seemed at first quite petrified by his profligacy. However, when the universal horror and displeasure had found a vent in ejaculations and execrations, he seemed to take even increased delight in his own lawless conduct, and was not to be controlled by his companions.

But in the midst of his most daring defiance, he suddenly uttered a cry of mingled rage and anguish; and after one violent effort to break his

9

chains, suddenly sank down powerless, with his head bowed on his breast and his eyes closed.

The reason of this transformation was soon evident to me. The cart had passed the men, and reached the part of the procession formed by the women. There stood Dinorah, pale as a corpse, her little hands convulsively clasped, her lips quivering, but with a look of the deepest sorrow in her eyes, as she fixed them upon the lost being before her. When this look met his, all his wild audacity was at once at an end.

The procession again put itself, singing, into motion, and was soon lost in a by-way behind the bushes; while the cart with the prisoner went on its way to Crozon, where I arrived soon after it, but was not able to remain. After a while, the newspapers gave me an account of Bauzec's execution.

Many years afterwards, on visiting a friend at Brest who occupied a position in its largest hospital, I recognized in one of the *Sœurs grises*, to whom the care of its sick was intrusted, the Virgin's god-daughter, Dinorah.

THE SEMPSTRESS' STORY

BY

GUSTAVE DROZ

From " The Sempstress' Story," by Gustave Droz.
Translated by E. T. D. Myers.   Published by
West, Johnston & Co.

THE SEMPSTRESS' STORY

BY GUSTAVE DROZ

" YES, Ma'm'selle Adèle," said the semp-stress, the real happiness of this world is not so unevenly distributed after all." Louise, as she said this, took from the reserve in the bosom of her dress a lot of pins, and applied them deftly to the trimming of a skirt which I was hold-ing for her.

"A sufficiently comfortable doctrine," I an-swered, " but it does seem to me as if some peo-ple were born to live and to die unhappy."

"It is only folks who never find anybody to love enough ; and I think it 's nobody's fault but their own."

" But, my good Louise, would n't you have suf-fered much less last year, when you came so near losing your boy, if you had n't cared so much for him ? "

I was only drawing her on, you see : Louise's chat was the greatest resource to me at that time.

"Why, Ma'm'selle Adèle, you are surely joking.

You 'd as well tell me to cut off my feet to save my shoes. You 'll know one of these days—and not so far off neither, maybe—how mighty easy and sensible it would be not to love your children. They *are* a worry, too ; but oh, the delight of 'em ! I 'd like to have had anybody tell me not to love my darling because it might grieve me, when he lay there in his mother's lap, with blue lips, gasping for his breath, and wellnigh dead ; his face blackish, and his hands like this piece of wax. You could see that everything was going against him ; and with his great big eyes he was staring in my face, until I felt as if the child was tugging at my very heartstrings. I kept smiling at him, though, through the tears that blinded me, hard as I tried to hide them. Oh ! such tears are bitter salt indeed, ma'm'selle ! And there was my poor husband on his knees, making paper figures to amuse him, and singing a funny song he used to laugh at. Now and then the corners of his mouth would pucker, and his cheeks would wrinkle a little bit under the eyes. You could tell he was still amused, but in such a dreamy way. Oh ! our child seemed no longer with us, but behind a veil, like. Wait a minute. You must excuse me, for I can't help crying when I think of it."

And the poor creature drew out her handkerchief and fairly sobbed aloud. In the midst of it, however, she smiled and said, " Well, that 's

over now; 't was nothing, and I 'm too silly.
And, ma'm'selle, here I 've gone and cried upon
your mother's dress, and that's a pretty business."

I took her hand in mine and pressed it.

" Are n't you afraid you 'll stick yourself,
ma'm'-selle ?   I 've got my needle in that hand,"
she said playfully.   " But you did not mean what
you said just now, did you ? "

" What did I say ? "

" That it would be better not to love your
children with all your heart, on account of the
great anxiety.   Don't you know such thoughts
are wicked ?   When they come into your head
your mind wants purifying.   But I 'm sure I beg
your pardon for saying so."

" You are entirely right, Louise," I returned.

" Ah ! so I thought.   And now, let me see.
Let 's fix this ruche ; pull it to the left a little,
please."

" But about the sick boy.   Tell me about his
recovery."

" That was a miracle—I ought to say two
miracles.   It was a miracle that God restored
him to us, and a miracle to find anybody with
so much knowledge and feeling,—such talent.
Such a tender heart, and so much, so much !—
I 'm speaking of the doctor.   A famous one he
was, too, you must know ; for it was no less than
Doctor Faron.   Heaven knows how he is run

after; and how rich and celebrated he is! Are n't
you surprised to hear that it was he who attended *our* little boy? Indeed, the wonders be-
gin with that. You may imagine my husband
was at his wits' end when he saw how it was
with the child; and all of a sudden I saw him
jump up, get out his best coat and hat, and put
them on."

"'Where are you going?' I asked.

"'To bring Doctor Faron.'

"Why, if he had said, 'To bring the Prime
Minister,' it would have seemed as likely.

"'Don't you believe Doctor Faron is going
to trouble himself about such as we. They will
turn you out of doors.'

" But 'twas no use talking, my dear. He was
already on the stairs, and I heard him running
away as if the house was on fire. Fire, indeed;
worse, far worse than any fire!

"And there I was, left alone with the child
upon my knees. He would n't stay in bed; and
was quieter so, wrapped up in his little blanket.
Here will he die, I thought. Soon will his eyes
close, and then it will be all over; and I held my
own breath to listen to his feeble and oppressed
pantings.

"About an hour had passed, when I heard a
rapid step on the stairs—(we are poor, and live
in attic rooms). The door opened, and my husband came in, wet with perspiration and out of

breath. If I live a century I'll not forget his look when he said :

"'Well?'

"I answered, 'No worse. But the doctor?'

"'He's coming.'

"Oh! those blessed words! It actually seemed as if my child were saved already. If you but knew how folks love their little ones. I kissed the darling, I kissed his father, I laughed, I cried, and I no longer felt the faintest doubt. It is by God's mercy that such gleams of hope are sent to strengthen us in our trials. It was very foolish, too; for something might easily have prevented the doctor's coming, after all.

"'You found him at home, then?' I inquired of my husband.

"Then he told me, in an undertone, what he had done, stopping every now and then to wipe his face and gather breath :

"'I ran to the Children's Hospital, which he manages, hoping to find him there. The porter showed me a low door at the end of the court-yard. I knocked and was let into a room full of young fellows, all smoking, talking and laughing away at a great rate.'

"Ah! the wretches! and with dying folks all round 'em."

"Don't say that until you know all. 'What do you want here, friend?' says a tall one in a white apron and black sleeves, and who, seeing my troubled looks, took me on one side. 'What's the matter?'

" 'I'm sorry to trouble you, sir,' I began.

" 'No ceremony, man. Speak out.'

" 'I'm looking for Doctor Faron, to come and save my child, sir. He's dying with croup. I'm not rich, but all I can raise I will give.'

" 'Oh! that's all right,' says he. 'How old's the child.'

" 'Four years old, sir.'

" 'Who's been attending it?'

" 'A doctor who gives him little white pills in a heap of water, sir.'

" 'Ah! hah!' says he, smiling; 'well, don't be downhearted,' and with that he threw off his apron and black sleeves, and wrote something on a bit of paper.'

"Take this to Doctor Faron. That's his address. Where do you live? I'll come when I get my coat on.'

" 'Oh! how kind, sir!'

"I could have hugged him. But he said, 'Come, no nonsense, friend. Away with you!' So I hurried off to Doctor Faron's house, with the note; but he was dining out.

" 'Where?' I asked, as the servant held the door ajar.

" 'Don't know,' says he, very short; and shut the door in my face.

" At that I got angry, and it seemed to me the

child came before my eyes. I pushed open the door, and in I went.

"'That won't do,' I said. 'One of the hospital doctors sent me here, and I *must* know where to find your master, and quick, too.'

"Seeing that I wouldn't stand trifling, he gave me the direction, and growled, 'Now clear out, and shut that door.'

"So I rushed away to the Rue de Lille. The courtyard was full of carriages, and the windows all in a blaze of light; but in I went, for all that.

"'My boy will die!—my boy will die!' I kept repeating, as I elbowed through the people. An old servant stopped me in the ante-chamber. 'Where now?' says he.

"'I want to speak to Doctor Faron,' says I; 'I *must* speak to him. Get him to come out here, won't you, please?'

"The old fellow looked at me hard, and then said very kindly, 'Sit down there an instant, and I'll try.'

"What possessed me to sit there and cry, with all those servants hurrying about with plates and dishes, I can't tell; but I could n't help it.

"In a minute or so, here comes a large gentleman with a white cravat on. 'Where's the man that wants me?' he asks in a gruff voice. Then seeing me there in the corner in such a state, with a searching look at me, he took the note,

read it, and said quietly, 'Ah! the noble boy.'
Then, turning to me, 'Go home, my man; I'll
be there directly. Cheer up; I'll lose no
time.'"

"My husband had scarcely uttered these
words," continued Louise, "when I heard a step
on the stairs. It was he! it was that blessed
angel of a doctor come to help us in our sore
distress.

"And what do you think he said in his deep
voice when he got into the room?

"'God bless you, my friends, but I nearly
broke my neck on those stairs. Where's that
child?'

"'Here he is, my dear, darling doctor.' I
knew no better way to speak to him, with his
dress-cravat showing over his great coat, and his
decorations dangling like a little bunch of keys
at his buttonhole.

"He took off his wrappings, stooped over the
child, turned him over, more gently even than
his mother could have done, and laid his own
head first against his back, then against his
breast. How I tried to read his eyes! but they
know how to hide their thoughts.

"'We must perform an operation here,' says
he; 'and it is high time.'

"Just at this moment the hospital doctor came
in, and whispered to him, 'I am afraid you
did n't want to be disturbed, sir.'

"Oh, never mind. I am sorry it was n't sooner, though. Get everything ready now.'

"But, Ma'm'selle Adèle, why should I tell you all this? I 'd better mind my work."

"Oh! go on, Louise, go on!"

"Well, then, ma'm'selle, if you believe me, those two doctors—neither of 'em kin, or even friends till then—went to work and made all the preparations, while my husband went off to borrow lights. The biggest one tied a mattress on the table, and the assistant spread out the bright little knives.

"You, who have not been through it all, ma'm'-selle, can 't know what it is to have your own little one in your lap, to know that those things are to be used upon him, to pierce his tender flesh, and, if the hand that guides them be not sure, that they may kill him.

"When all was ready, Doctor Faron took off his cravat, then lifted my child from my arms and laid him on the mattress, in the midst of the lamps, and said to my poor man :

" ' You will hold his head, and your wife his feet. Joseph will pass me the instruments. You 've brought a breathing tube with you, my son?'

" ' Yes, sir.'

"My husband was as white as a sheet by this ; and when I saw him about to take his place with his hands shaking so much, it scared me, so I said :

"'Doctor, please let me hold his head!'

"'But, my poor woman, if you should tremble?'

"'Please let me do it, Doctor!'

"'Be it so then,' and then added, with a bright look at me, and a cheering smile, 'we shall save him for you, my dear; you are a brave little woman, and you deserve it.'

"Yes, and save him, did he! God bless him! saved him as truly as if he had snatched him from the depths of the river."

"And you did n't tremble, Louise?"

"You may depend on that. If I had, it would have been the last of my child."

"How in the world did you keep yourself steady?"

"The Lord knows; but I was like a rock. When you must, you must, I suppose."

"And you had to behold every detail of that operation?"

"Yes, indeed; and often have I dreamed it over since. His poor little neck laid open, and the veins, which the doctor pushed aside with his fingers and the little silver tube which he inserted, and all that; and then the face of the child, changing as the air passed into his lungs. You 've seen a lamp almost out, when you pour in oil? It was like that. They had laid him there but half alive, with his eyes all but set; and they gave him back to me, pale and with bloodless lips, it is true, but with life in his looks, and breathing—breathing the free, fresh air.

" ' Kiss him, mother,' says the doctor, ' and put him to bed. Cover the place with some light thing or other, and Joseph must stay with you to-night ; won't you, Joseph ? Ah, well, that 's all arranged.'

" He put on his things and wrapped himself up to go. He was shaking hands with my husband, when I seized one hand, and kissed it—like a fool, as I was—but I did n't stop to think. He laughed heartily, and said to my husband, ' Are you not jealous, friend ? Your wife is making great advances to me. But I must be off now. Good-night, good people.'

" And from that night he always talks so friendly and familiarly to us, not a bit contempt-uously either, but as if he liked us, and was glad to be of service to us.

" The next morning, at half-past five, there he was, as fresh as a rose, and larger, as it seemed to me, than before. And no wonder, neither, for don't you think he had brought four bottles of old Bordeaux ! two in his pockets and two under his arms.

" ' The little fellow must take this,' says he. ' Everything gone on well in the night, eh ?'

" ' Admirably well, sir,' answered Mr. Joseph. I call him Mr. Joseph, but I have since found

out that he was a rising physician, nephew to
the old doctor, and 'way above the common run.
But he always spoke to the other like a soldier
to his general.

"Well, that's not all the doctor did; for during the entire week after, he came every day,
and when I would hear his carriage rumbling
over our poor little street, I would say, ' Heaven
knows what we shall ever do to pay him.' For
we well knew that Doctor Faron attended dukes
and noblemen, and charged them by the thousand.

"We had some hundred francs in the Savings,
to be sure, but I was thinking what we should
do if he charged two or three times as much.
You can understand how very awkward it would
have been. It fairly made me sick.

"At last, one morning when my husband was at
home, I mustered up all my courage and began:

"'Doctor Faron, you have been so good, too
good to us. You have saved our boy's life.'

"'You may prate over that just as much as
you please, my dear; but recollect it is my trade
to cut up such little chaps.'

"'But not those who live *au cinquième* in the
Rue Serpente, sir.'

"You see, ma'm'selle, how I was leading up
to the question?

"'How's that? how's that? Why, what are
you talking about? Those before anybody else,
to be sure. Are they not most in need?'

" ' I know you have the best heart in the world, doctor; but that 's not what I mean. Now, that the child is well, we want to—we are not rich— but still—'

" By this time I was as red as a cock's comb, and the more I tried to express myself the worse it got.

" ' You want to pay me. I see, I see,' said he suddenly. ' Well, you owe me precisely nothing, if you don't think that too much.'

" ' Oh! doctor! we could n't—we must—'

" ' Let us pay according to our means, doctor,' says my husband.

" Well, then, I don't want to wound you, my friends. If you prefer to pay something, my charge is just fifty francs. And now don't bother me any more about it. (He pretended to be angry, and it was so droll.) Don't bother me, I say, you lunatics. Fifty francs, I tell you, and not a copper less; in specie, too; no paper money for me. Next Sunday dress the little man, and have him ready; for I wish him to take a turn in the Bois de Boulogne.'

" Ah! there 's no end to your kindness, doctor.'

" ' Do n't interrupt me, I say. After his drive, bring him to see me; and let him fetch the money himself. Do you hear ?'

" Well, ma'm'selle," added Louise, " that very evening here comes a basket of wine, although we had n't finished the other. What a man!

10

you may well say. And I declare to you, if he had wanted my right arm, I should have said, 'Cut it off, sir.'

"Fifty francs, indeed! It was n't the twentieth of what we owed him; and he only took that to save our feelings. And seeing this, I was still more anxious to please him; so I bought some linen, the finest I could get, and did n't I make him an elegant set of shirts!"

"Why, how did you get his measure?"

"Ah! that *was* hard; but when I make up my mind nothing stops me. I went to his valet—who knew me, because he had brought the wine —and I told him the doctor wanted me to look over his linen in the wash. So I got to the laundress, and I made her think he had ordered some shirts like those she had in hand, and so I got the pattern.

"I was full of work at that time, but I made all those shirts at night; and it gave me such satisfaction to think, 'Ah! you won't let us pay you—you obstinate man—but you can't prevent my sitting up and working for you the livelong night; and the way I worked! you should have seen me at it!

"You may depend on it there was plenty of hemstitching on those shirts, and you know when I try I *can* hemstitch.

"But I am trifling away my time, and this dress will never be done,"

THE VENUS OF ILLE

BY

PROSPER MÉRIMÉE

THE VENUS OF ILLE

Γλεὼς ἦν δὲγὼ, ἔστω ὁ ἀνδρίας
καὶ ἤπιος, οὕτως ἀνδρεῖος ὤν.
Δουκιανου Φιλοψευδης.

BY PROSPER MÉRIMÉE

I WAS descending the last slope of the Canigou, and though the sun was already set I could distinguish on the plain the houses of the small town of Ille, towards which I directed my steps.

" Of course," I said to the Catalan who since the day before served as my guide, " you know where M. de Peyrehorade lives ? "

" Just don't I! " cried he ; " I know his house like my own, and if it were not so dark I would show it to you. It is the finest in Ille. He is rich, M. de Peyrehorade is, and he marries his son to one richer even than he."

" Does the marriage come off soon ? " I asked him.

" Soon ? It may be that the violins are already ordered for the wedding. To-night perhaps, to-morrow, or the next day, how do I know ?

It will take place at Puygarrig, for it is Mademoiselle de Puygarrig that the son is to marry. It will be a sight, I can tell you."

I was recommended to M. de Peyrehorade by my friend M. de P. He was, I had been told, an antiquarian of much learning and a man of charming affability. He would take delight in showing me the ruins for ten leagues around. Therefore I counted on him to visit the outskirts of Ille, which I knew to be rich in memorials of the Middle Ages. This marriage, of which I now heard for the first time, upset all my plans.

"I shall be a troublesome guest, I told myself. But I am expected; my arrival has been announced by M. de P.; I must present myself."

When we reached the plain the guide said, "Wager a cigar, sir, that I can guess what you are going to do at M. de Peyrehorade's."

Offering him one, I answered: "It is not very hard to guess. At this hour, when one has made six leagues in the Canigou, supper is the great thing after all."

"Yes, but to-morrow? Here I wager that you have come to Ille to see the idol. I guessed that when I saw you draw the portraits of the saints at Serrabona."

"The idol! what idol?" This word had aroused my curiosity.

"What! were you not told at Perpignan how

M. de Peyrehorade had found an idol in the earth ? ”

“ You mean to say an earthen statue ? ”

“ Not at all. A statue in copper, and there is enough of it to make a lot of big pennies. She weighs as much as a church-bell. It was deep in the ground at the foot of an olive tree that we got her.”

“ You were present at the discovery ? ”

“ Yes, sir. Two weeks ago M. de Peyrehorade told Jean Coll and me to uproot an old olive tree which was frozen last year when the weather as you know was very severe. So in working, Jean Coll, who went at it with all his might, gave a blow with his pickaxe, and I heard *bimm*—as if he had struck a bell, and I said, What is that ? We dug on and on, and there was a black hand, which looked like the hand of a corpse, sticking out of the earth. I was scared to death. I ran to M. de Peyrehorade and I said to him, ‘There are dead people, master, under the olive tree ! The priest must be called.’

“ ‘What dead people ?’ said he to me. He came, and he had no sooner seen the hand, than he cried out ‘An antique ! an antique !’ You would have thought he had found a treasure. And there he was with the pickaxe in his own hands, struggling and doing almost as much work as we two.”

“ And at last what did you find ? ”

"A huge black woman more than half naked, with due respect to you, sir. She was all in copper, and M. de Peyrehorade told us it was an idol of pagan times—the time of Charlemagne."

"I see what it is,—some virgin or other in bronze from a destroyed convent."

"A virgin! Had it been one I should have recognized it. It is an idol, I tell you; you can see it in her look. She fixes you with her great white eyes—one might say she stares at you. One lowers one's eyes, yes indeed one does, on looking at her."

"White eyes? Doubtless they are set in the bronze. Perhaps it is some Roman statue."

"Roman! That's it. M. de Peyrehorade says it is Roman. Oh! I see you are an erudite like himself."

"Is she complete, well preserved?"

"Yes, sir, she lacks nothing. It is a handsomer statue and better finished than the bust of Louis Philippe in colored plaster which is in the town-hall. But with all that the face of the idol does not please me. She has a wicked expression,—and, what is more, she is wicked."

"Wicked! what has she done to you?"

"Nothing to me exactly; but wait a minute. We had gotten down on all-fours to stand her upright, and M. de Peyrehorade was also pull-

ing on the rope, though he has not much more
strength than a chicken. With much trouble we
got her up straight. I reached for a broken tile
to support her, when if she does n't tumble over
backwards all in a heap. I said, 'Take care,'
but not quick enough, for Jean did not have time
to draw away his leg—"

"And it was hurt?"

"Broken as clean as a vine-prop. When I
saw that I was furious, I wanted to take my pickaxe and smash the statue to pieces, but M. de
Peyrehorade stopped me. He gave Jean Coll
some money, but all the same, he is in bed still,
though it is two weeks since it happened, and the
physician says that he will never walk as well
with that leg as with the other. It is a pity, for
he was our best runner, and, after M. de Peyrehorade's son, the cleverest racquet player. M.
Alphonse de Peyrehorade was sorry I can tell
you, for Coll always played on his side. It was
beautiful to see how they returned each other the
balls. They never touched the ground."

Chatting in this way we entered Ille, and I
soon found myself in the presence of M. de Peyrehorade. He was a little old man, still hale
and active, with powdered hair, a red nose, and
a jovial, bantering manner. Before opening M.
de P.'s letter he had seated me at a well-spread
table, and had presented me to his wife and son
as a celebrated archæologist who was to draw

Roussillon from the neglect in which the indifference of erudites had left it.

While eating heartily—for nothing makes one hungrier than the keen air of the mountains—I scrutinized my hosts. I have said a word about M. de Peyrehorade, I must add that he was activity personified. He talked, got up, ran to his library, brought me books, showed me engravings, and filled my glass, all at the same time. He was never two minutes in repose. His wife was a trifle stout, as are most Catalans when they are over forty years of age. She appeared to me a thorough provincial, solely occupied with her housekeeping. Though the supper was sufficient for at least six persons, she hurried to the kitchen and had pigeons killed and a number broiled, and she opened I do not know how many jars of preserves. In no time the table was laden with dishes and bottles, and if I had but tasted of everything offered me I should certainly have died of indigestion. Nevertheless, at each dish I refused they made fresh excuses. They feared I found myself very badly off at Ille. In the provinces there were so few resources, and of course Parisians were fastidious!

In the midst of his parents' comings and goings M. Alphonse de Peyrehorade was as immovable as rent-day. He was a tall young man of twenty-six with a regular and handsome countenance, but lacking in expression. His height and his athletic figure well justified the reputation of an indefatigable racquet player given him in the neighborhood.

On that evening he was dressed in an elegant manner ; that is to say, he was an exact copy of a fashion plate in the last number of the *Journal des Modes*. But he seemed to me ill at ease in his clothes ; he was as stiff as a post in his velvet collar, and could only turn all of a piece. In striking contrast to his costume were his large sunburnt hands and blunt nails. They were a laborer's hands issuing from the sleeves of an exquisite. Moreover, though he examined me in my quality of Parisian most curiously from head to foot, he only spoke to me once during the whole evening, and that was to ask me where I had bought my watch-chain.

As the supper was drawing to an end M. de Peyrehorade said to me : " Ah ! my dear guest, you belong to me now you are here. I shall not let go of you until you have seen everything of interest in our mountains. You must learn to know our Roussillon, and to do it justice. You do not suspect all that we have to show you.— Phœnician, Celtic, Roman, Arabian, and Byzantine monuments ; you shall see them all from the cedar to the hyssop. I shall drag you everywhere, and will not spare you a single stone."

A fit of coughing obliged him to pause. I took advantage of it to tell him that I should be sorry to disturb him on an occasion of so much interest to his family.   If he would but give me his excellent advice about the excursions to be made, I could manage, without his taking the trouble to accompany me.

"Ah! you mean the marriage of that boy there," he exclaimed, interrupting me; "stuff and nonsense, it will be over the day after to-morrow.   You will go to the wedding with us, which is to be informal, as the bride is in mourning for an aunt whose heiress she is.   Therefore, there will be no festivities, no ball.   It is a pity, though ; you might have seen our Catalans dance. They are pretty, and might have given you the desire to imitate Alphonse.   One marriage, they say, leads to another.   Once the young people married I shall be free, and we will bestir ourselves.   I beg your pardon for boring you with a provincial wedding.   For a Parisian tired of entertainments—and a wedding without a ball at that !   Still you will see a bride—a bride—well, you shall tell me what you think of her.   But you are a thinker and no longer notice women. I have better than that to show you.   You shall see something ; in fact, I have a fine surprise in store for you to-morrow."

"Good heavens!" said I; "it is difficult to have a treasure in the house without the public being aware of it.   I think I know the surprise in reserve for me.   But if it is your statue which is in question, the description my guide gave me of it has only served to excite my curiosity and prepared me to admire."

"Ah! So he spoke to you about the idol, as he calls my beautiful Venus Tur; but I will tell you nothing. To-morrow you shall see her by daylight, and tell me if I am right in thinking the statue a masterpiece. You could not have arrived more opportunely. There are inscriptions on it which I, poor ignoramus that I am, explain after my own fashion; but you, a Parisian erudite, will probably laugh at my interpretation; for I have actually written a paper about it,—I, an old provincial antiquary, have launched myself in literature. I wish to make the press groan. If you would kindly read and correct it I might have some hope. For example, I am very anxious to know how you translate this inscription from the base of the statue: CAVE. But I do not wish to ask you yet! Wait until to-morrow. Not a word more ahout the Venus to-day!"

"You are right, Peyrehorade," said his wife; "drop your idol. Can you not see that you prevent our guest from eating? You may be sure that he has seen in Paris much finer statues than yours. In the Tuilleries there are dozens, and they also are in bronze."

"There you have the saintly ignorance of the provinces!" interrupted M. de Peyrehorade.

"The idea of comparing an admirable antique
to the insipid figures of Coustou !

> 'How irreverently my housekeeper
>   Speaks of the gods!'

Do you know that my wife wanted me to melt my
statue into a bell for our church.   She would
have been the godmother.   Just think of it, to
melt a masterpiece by Myron, sir!"

"Masterpiece !   Masterpiece !   A charming
masterpiece she is ! to break a man's leg."

"Madam, do you see that?" said M. de Peyrehorade in a resolute tone, extending toward her
his right leg in its changeable silk stocking; "if
my Venus had broken that leg there for me I
should not regret it."

"Good gracious !   Peyrehorade, how can you
say such a thing !   Fortunately, the man is better.
And yet I cannot bring myself to look at a statue
which has caused so great a disaster.   Poor Jean
Coll !"

"Wounded by Venus, sir," said M. de Peyrehorade, with a loud laugh ; "wounded by Venus,
and the churl complains !

> 'Veneris nec præmia nôris.'

Who has not been wounded by Venus?"

M. Alphonse, who understood French better
than Latin, winked one eye with an air of intel-
ligence, and looked at me as if to ask, "And you,
Parisian, do you understand?"

The supper came to an end. I had ceased
eating an hour before. I was weary, and I could
not manage to hide the frequent yawns which
escaped me. Madame de Peyrehorade was the
first to notice them, and remarked that it was
time to go to bed. Then followed fresh apologies for the poor accommodations I would have.
I would not be as well off as in Paris. It was
so uncomfortable in the provinces ! Indulgence
was needed for the Roussillonnais. Notwithstanding my protests that after a tramp in the
mountains a bundle of straw would seem to me a
delicious couch, they continued begging me to
pardon poor country people if they did not treat
me as well as they could have wished.

Accompanied by M. de Peyrehorade I ascended
at last to the room arranged for me. The stair-
case, the upper half of which was in wood, ended
in the centre of a hall, out of which opened
several rooms.

"To the right," said my host, "is the apartment which I propose to give the future Madame
Alphonse. Your room is at the opposite end of
the corridor. You understand," he added in a
manner which he meant to be sly,—" you understand that newly married people must be alone.
You are at one end of the house, they at the
other."

We entered a well-furnished room where the
first object on which my gaze rested was a bed

seven feet long, six wide, and so high that one needed a chair to climb up into it.

Having shown me where the bell was, and assured himself that the sugar-bowl was full and the cologne bottles duly placed on the toilet-stand, my host asked me a number of times if anything was lacking, wished me good-night, and left me alone.

The windows were closed. Before undressing I opened one to breathe the fresh night air so delightful after a long supper. Facing me was the Canigou. Always magnificent, it appeared to me on that particular evening, lighted as it was by a resplendent moon, as the most beautiful mountain in the world. I remained a few minutes contemplating its marvellous silhouette, and was about to close the window when, lowering my eyes, I perceived a dozen yards from the house, the statue on its pedestal. It was placed at the corner of a hedge that separated a small garden from a vast, perfectly level quadrangle, which I learned later was the racquet court of the town. This ground was the property of M. de Peyrehorade, and had been given by him to the parish at the solicitation of his son.

Owing to the distance it was difficult for me to distinguish the attitude of the statue ; I could only judge of its height, which seemed to be about six feet. At that moment two scamps of the town, whistling the pretty Roussillon tune, *Mon-*

tagnes régalades, were crossing the racquet court quite near the hedge. They paused to look at the statue, and one of them even apostrophized it aloud. He spoke Catalonian, but I had been long enough in Roussillon to understand pretty well what he said.

"There you are, you wench!" (The Catalonian word was much more forcible.) "There you are!" he said. "It was you then who broke Jean Coll's leg! If you belonged to me I'd break your neck."

"Bah! what with?" said the other youth. "It is of the copper of pagan times, and harder than I don't know what."

"If I had my chisel" (it seems he was a locksmith's apprentice), "I would soon force out its big white eyes, as I would pop an almond from its shell. There are more than a hundred pennies' worth of silver in them."

They went on a few steps.

"I must wish the idol good-night," said the taller of the apprentices, stopping suddenly.

He stooped and probably picked up a stone. I saw him unbend his arm and throw something. A blow resounded on the bronze, and immediately the apprentice raised his hand to his head with a cry of pain.

"She threw it back at me!" he exclaimed. And my two rascals ran off as fast as they could. It was evident that the stone had rebounded

11

from the metal and had punished the wag for the
outrage he had done the goddess. Laughing
heartily, I shut the window.

Another Vandal punished by Venus! May all
the desecrators of our old monuments thus get
their due!

With this charitable wish I fell asleep.

When I awoke it was broad day. On one side
of my bed stood M. de Peyrehorade in a dressing-
gown; a servant sent by his wife was on the
other side with a cup of chocolate in his hand.

"Come, come, you Parisian, get up! This is
qnite the laziness of the capital!" said my host,
while I dressed in haste. "It is eight o'clock,
and you are still in bed! I have been up since
six. This is the third time I have been to your
door. I approached on tiptoe: no one, not a
sign of life. It is bad for you to sleep too much
at your age. And my Venus, which you have
not yet seen! Come, hurry up and take this cup
of Barcelona chocolate. It is real contraband
chocolate, such as cannot be found in Paris. Pre-'
pare yourself, for when you are once before my
Venus no one will be able to tear you away from
her."

I was ready in five minutes; that is to say, I
was half shaved, half dressed, and burned by the
boiling chocolate I had swallowed. I descended
to the garden and saw an admirable statue before me. It was truly a Venus, and of marvel-

lous beauty. The upper part of the body was nude, as great divinities were usually represented by the ancients. The right hand was raised as high as the breast, the palm turned inwards, the thumb and two first fingers extended, and the others slightly bent. The other hand, drawn close to the hip, held the drapery which covered the lower half of the body. The attitude of this statue reminded one of that of the *mourre* player which is called, I hardly know why, by the name of Germanicus. Perhaps it had been intended to represent the goddess as playing at *mourre*. However that may be, it is impossible to find anything more perfect than the form of this Venus, anything softer and more voluptuous than her outlines, or more graceful and dignified than her drapery. I had expected a work of the decadence; I saw a masterpiece of statuary's best days.

What struck me most was the exquisite reality of the figure; one might have thought it moulded from life, that is, if Nature ever produced such perfect models.

The hair, drawn back from the brow, seemed once to have been gilded. The head was small, like nearly all those of Greek statues, and bent slightly forward. As to the face, I shall never succeed in describing its strange character; it was of a type belonging to no other Greek statue which I can remember. It had not the calm, severe beauty of the Greek sculptors, who systematically gave a majestic immobility to all the features. On the contrary, I noticed here, with surprise, a marked intention on the artist's part to reproduce malice verging on viciousness. All the features were slightly contracted. The eyes were rather oblique, the mouth raised at the corners, the nostrils a trifle dilated. Disdain, irony, and cruelty were to be read in the nevertheless beautiful face.

Truly, the more one gazed at the statue the more one experienced a feeling of pain that such wonderful beauty could be allied to such an absence of all sensibility.

"If the model ever existed," I said to M. de Peyrehorade, "and I doubt if heaven ever produced such a woman, how I pity her lovers! She must have taken pleasure in making them die of despair. There is something ferocious in her expression, and yet I have never seen anything more beautiful."

"' C'est Venus tout entière à sa proie attachée!'" cried M. de Peyrehorade, delighted with my enthusiasm.

But the expression of demoniac irony was perhaps increased by the contrast of the bright silver eyes with the dusky green hue which time had given to the statue. The shining eyes produced a sort of illusion which simulated reality and life. I remembered what my guide had said, that those who looked at her were forced to lower their eyes. It was almost true, and I could not prevent a movement of anger at myself when I felt ill at ease before this bronze figure.

"Now that you have seen everything in detail, my dear colleague in antiquities, let us, if you please, open a scientific conference. What do you say to this inscription which you have not yet noticed?" He pointed to the base of the statue, and I read these words:

CAVE AMANTEM.

"*Quid dicis doctissime?*" he asked, rubbing his hands. "Let us see if we agree as to the meaning of *cave amantem!*"

"But," I replied, "it has two meanings. You can translate it: 'Guard against him who loves thee,' that is, 'distrust lovers.' But in this sense I do not know if *cave amantem* would be good Latin. After seeing the diabolical expression of the lady I should sooner believe that the artist meant to warn the spectator against this terrible beauty. I should then translate it: 'Take care of thyself if *she* loves thee.'"

"Humph!" said M. de Peyrehorade; "yes, it is an admissible meaning: but, if you do not mind, I prefer the first translation, which I would, however, develop. You know Venus's lover?"

"There are several."

"Yes; but the first is Vulcan. Why should

it not mean : 'Notwithstanding all thy beauty, thine air of disdain, thou wilt have a blacksmith, a wretched cripple for a lover'? A profound lesson, sir, for coquettes!"

The explication seemed so far-fetched that I could not help smiling.

To avoid formally contradicting my antiquarian friend, I observed, "Latin is a terrible language in its conciseness," and I drew back several steps to better contemplate the statue.

"Wait a moment, colleague!" said M. de Peyrehorade, catching hold of my arm; "you have not seen all. There is another inscription. Climb up on the pedestal and look at the right arm." So saying, he helped me up, and without much ceremony I clung to the neck of the Venus with whom I was becoming more familiar. For a second I even looked her straight in the eyes, and on close inspection she appeared more wicked, and, if possible, more beautiful than before. Then I noticed that on the arm were engraved, as it seemed to me, characters in ancient script. With the aid of my spectacles I spelt out what follows, and M. de Peyrehorade, approving with voice and gesture, repeated each word as I uttered it. Thus I read:

VENERI TVRBVL .
EVTVCHES MYRO.
IMPERIO FECIT.

After the word "Tvrbvl" in the first line it looked to me as if there were several letters effaced ; but " Tvrbvl " was perfectly legible.

"Which means to say?" my host asked radiantly, with a mischievous smile, for he thought the " Tvrbvl " would puzzle me.

"There is one word which I do not yet understand," I answered; "all the rest is simple. Eutyches Myron has made this offering to Venus by her command."

"Quite right. But 'Tvrbvl,' what do you make of it? What does it mean ?"

"'Tvrbvl' perplexes me very much. I am trying to think of one of Venus's familiar characteristics which may enlighten me. But what do you say to 'Tvrbvlenta'? The Venus who troubles, agitates. You see I am still preoccupied by her wicked expression. 'Tvrbvlenta' is not too bad a quality for Venus," I added modestly, for I was not too well satisfied with my explanation.

"A turbulent Venus! A noisy Venus! Ah! then you think my Venus is a public-house Venus? Nothing of the kind, sir; she is a Venus of good society. I will explain ' Tvrbvl ' to you—that is, if you promise me not to divulge my discovery before my article appears in print. Because, you see, I pride myself on such a find, and, after all, you Parisian erudites are rich enough to leave a few ears for us poor devils of provincials to glean !"

From the top of the pedestal, where I was still perched, I promised him solemnly that I would never be so base as to filch from him his discovery.

"'Tvrbvl,'—sir," said he, coming nearer and lowering his voice for fear some one besides myself might hear him, "read 'Tvrbvlneræ.'"

"I understand no better."

"Listen to me attentively. Three miles from here at the foot of the mountain is a village called Boulternère. The name is a corruption of the Latin word 'Tvrbvlnera.' Nothing is more common than these transpositions. Boulternère was a Roman town. I always suspected it, but I could get no proof till now, and here it is. This Venus was the local goddess of the city of Boulternère; and the word Boulternère, which I have shown is of ancient origin, proves something very curious, namely, that Boulternère was a Phœnician town before it was Roman!"

He paused a moment to take breath and enjoy my surprise. I succeeded in overcoming a strong inclination to laugh.

"'Tvrbvlnera' is, in fact, pure Phœnician," he continued. "'Tvr,' pronounce 'tour'—'Tour' and 'Sour' are the same word, are they not? 'Sour' is the Phœnician name of Tyr; I do not need to recall the meaning to you. 'Bvl' is Baal; Bâl, Bel, Bul, are slight differences of pronunciation. As to 'Nera,' that troubles me a little. I am tempted to believe, for want of a Phœnician word, that it comes from the Greek νηρός, moist, marshy. In that case, it is a mongrel word. To justify νηρός I will show you at Boulternère how the mountain streams form stagnant pools. Then, again, the ending ' Nera ' may have been added much later in honor of Nera Pivesuvia, wife of Tetricus, who may have benefited the city of Turbul. But on account of the marshes, I prefer the etymology of νηρός."

He took a pinch of snuff in a complacent way, and continued:

" But let us leave the Phœnicians and return to the inscription. I translate it then : To Venus of Boulternère Myron dedicates by her order this statue, his work."

I took good care not to criticise his etymology, but I wished in my turn to give a proof of penetration, so I said :

" Stop a moment, M. de Peyrehorade. Myron has dedicated something, but I by no means see that it is this statue."

" What ! " he cried, " was not Myron a famous Greek sculptor ? The talent was perpetuated in his family, and it must have been one of his descendants who executed this statue. Nothing can be more certain."

" But," I replied, " on this arm I see a small hole. I think it served to fasten something—a bracelet, for example—which this Myron, being an unhappy lover, gave to Venus as an expiatory offering. Venus was irritated against him; he appeased her by consecrating to her a gold bracelet. Notice that *fecit* is often used for *consecravit*. The terms are synonymous. I could show you more than one example if I had at hand Gruter or Orellius. It is natural that a lover should see Venus in a dream and imagine that she commands him to give a gold bracelet to her statue. Myron consecrated the bracelet to her. Then the barbarians or some other sacrilegious thieves—"

"Ah! it is easy to see you have written romances!" cried my host, helping me down from the pedestal. "No, sir; it is a work of Myron's school. You have only to look at the workmanship to be convinced of that."

Having made it a rule never to contradict self-opinionated antiquarians, I bowed with an air of conviction, saying:

"It is an admirable piece of work."

"Good heavens!" exclaimed M. de Peyrehorade, "another act of vandalism! Some one must have thrown a stone at my statue!"

He had just perceived a white mark a little above the bosom of the Venus. I noticed a similar mark on the fingers of the right hand. I supposed it had been touched by the stone as it passed, or that a bit of the stone had been broken off as it struck the statue, and had rebounded on the hand. I told my host of the insult I had witnessed, and the prompt punishment which had followed it.

He laughed heartily, and, comparing the apprentice to Diomede, wished he might, like the Greek hero, see all his comrades turned into white birds.

The breakfast bell interrupted this classical conversation, and, as on the preceding evening, I was obliged to eat enough for four. Then came M. de Peyrehorade's farmers, and, while he was giving them an audience, his son led me to inspect an open carriage, which he had bought at Toulouse for his betrothed, and which it is needless to say I duly admired. After that I went into the stable with him, where he kept me a half-hour, boasting about his horses, giving me their genealogy, and telling me of the prizes they had won at the county races. At last he began to talk to me about his betrothed in connection with a gray mare which he intended for her.

"We will see her to-day," he said. "I do not know if you will find her pretty. In Paris people are hard to please. But every one here and in Perpignan thinks her lovely. The best of it is that she is very rich. Her aunt from Prades left her a fortune. Oh! I shall be very happy."

I was profoundly shocked to see a young man

appear more affected by the dower than by the beauty of his bride.

"You are a judge of jewels," continued M. Alphonse; "what do you think of this? Here is the ring I shall give her to-morrow."

He drew from his little finger a heavy ring, enriched with diamonds, and fashioned into two clasped hands, an allusion which seemed to me infinitely poetic. The workmanship was antique. but I fancied it had been retouched to insert the diamonds. Inside the ring these words in Gothic characters could be discerned: *Sempr' ab ti*, which means, thine for ever.

"It is a pretty ring," I said, "but the diamonds which have been added have made it lose a little of its style."

"Oh! it is much handsomer now," he answered, smiling. "There are twelve hundred francs' worth of diamonds in it. My mother gave it to me. It is a very old family ring,—it dates from the days of chivalry. It was my grandmother's, who had it from her grandmother. Heaven knows when it was made."

"The custom in Paris," I said, "is to give a perfectly plain ring, usually composed of two different metals, such as gold and platina. The other ring which you have on would be very suitable. This one with its diamonds and its clasped hands is so thick that it would be impossible to wear a glove over it."

" Madame Alphonse must arrange that as she pleases. I think she will be very glad to have it all the same. Twelve hundred francs on the finger is pleasant. That other little ring," he added, looking in a contented way at the plain ring he wore, "that one a woman in Paris gave me on Shrove Tuesday. How I did enjoy myself when I was in Paris two years ago! That is the place to have a good time !" and he sighed regretfully.

We were to dine that day at Puygarrig with the relations of the bride; so we got into the carriage, and drove to the château, which was four or five miles from Ille. I was presented and received as the friend of the family. I will not speak of the dinner, or the conversation which followed. I took but little part in it. M. Alphonse was seated beside his betrothed, and whispered a word or two in her ear now and then. As for her, she hardly raised her eyes; and every time her lover spoke to her she blushed modestly, but answered without embarrassment.

Mademoiselle de Puygarrig was eighteen years of age. Her slender, graceful figure formed a striking contrast to the stalwart frame of her future husband. She was not only beautiful, she was alluring. I admired the perfect naturalness of all her replies. Her kind look, which yet was not free from a touch of malice, reminded me, in spite of myself, of my host's Venus. While making this inward comparison, I asked myself if the incontestably superior beauty of the statue did not in great measure come from its tigress-like expression; for strength, even in evil passions, always arouses in us astonishment, and a sort of involuntary admiration.

"What a pity," I thought, on leaving Puygarrig, "that such an attractive girl should be rich, and that her dowry makes her sought by a man quite unworthy of her."

While returning to Ille, I spoke to Mme. de Peyrehorade, to whom I thought it only proper to address myself now and then, though I did not very well know what to say to her: "You must be strong-minded people in Roussillon," I said. "How is it, madam, that you have a wedding on a Friday? We would be more superstitious in Paris; no one would dare be married on that day."

"Do not speak of it," she replied: "if it had depended on me, certainly another day would have been chosen. But Peyreborade wished it, and I had to give in. All the same, it troubles me very much. Supposing an accident should happen? There must be some reason in it, or else why is every one afraid of Friday?"

"Friday!" cried her husband, "is Venus's day! Just the day for a wedding! You see, my dear colleague, I think only of my Venus.

I chose Friday on her account. To-morrow, if you like, before the wedding, we will make a little sacrifice to her—a sacrifice of two doves —and if I only knew where to get some incense—"

"For shame, Peyrehorade!" interrupted his wife, scandalized to the last degree. "Incense to an idol! It would be an abomination! What would they say of us in the neighborhood?"

"At least," answered M. de Peyrehorade, "you will allow me to place a wreath of roses and lilies on her head: *Manibus date lilia plenis.* You see, sir, freedom is an empty word. We have not liberty of worship!"

The next day's arrangements were ordered in the following manner: Every one was to be dressed and ready at ten o'clock punctually. After the chocolate had been served we were to be driven to Puygarrig. The civil marriage was to take place in the town-hall of the village, and the religious ceremony in the chapel of the château. Afterwards there would be a breakfast. After the breakfast people would pass the time as they liked until seven o'clock. At that hour every one would return to M. de Peyrehorade's at Ille, where the two families were to assemble and have supper. It was natural that being unable to dance they should wish to eat as much as possible.

By eight o'clock I was seated in front of the
Venus, pencil in hand, recommencing the head
of the statue for the twentieth time without
being able to catch the expression. M. de Peyrehorade came and went about me, giving me
advice, repeating his Phœnician etymology, and
laying Bengal roses on the pedestal of the statue
while he addressed vows to it in a tragi-comic
tone for the young couple who were to live under
his roof. Towards nine o'clock he went in to
put on his best, and at the same moment M.
Alphonse appeared looking very stiff in a new
coat, white gloves, chased sleeve-buttons, and
varnished shoes. A rose decorated his buttonhole.

"Will you make my wife's portrait?" he
asked, leaning over my drawing. "She also is
pretty."

On the racquet-court of which I have spoken
there now began a game which immediately attracted M. Alphonse's attention. And I, tired,
and despairing of ever being able to copy the
diabolical face, soon left my drawing to look at
the players. There were among them some
Spanish muleteers who had arrived the night before. They were from Aragon and Navarre, and
were nearly all marvellously skilful at the game.
Therefore the Illois, though encouraged by the
presence and advice of M. Alphonse, were
promptly beaten by the foreign champions. The

native spectators were disheartened. M. Alphonse looked at his watch. It was only half-past nine. His mother's hair he knew was not dressed. He hesitated no longer, but taking off his coat asked for a jacket, and defied the Spaniards. I looked on smiling and a little surprised. "The honor of the country must be sustained," he said.

Then I thought him really handsome. He seemed full of life, and his costume, which but now occupied him so entirely, no longer concerned him. A few minutes before he would have dreaded to turn his head for fear of disarranging his cravat. Now he did not give a thought to his curled hair or his fine shirt-front. And his betrothed? If it had been necessary I think he would have postponed the wedding. I saw him hurriedly put on a pair of sandals, roll up his sleeves, and, with an assured air, take his stand at the head of the vanquished party like Cæsar rallying his soldiers at Dyrrachium. I leaped the hedge and placed myself comfortably in the shade of a tree so as to command a good view of both sides.

Contrary to general expectation, M. Alphonse missed the first ball. It came skimming along the ground, it is true, and was thrown with astonishing force by an Aragonese who appeared to be the leader of the Spaniards.

He was a man of about forty, nervous and

12

agile, and at least six feet tall.   His olive skin
was almost as dark as the bronze of the Venus.

M. Alphonse threw his racquet angrily on the
ground.

"It is this cursed ring," he cried, "which
squeezes my finger, and makes me miss a sure
ball."

He drew off his diamond ring with some difficulty; I approached to take it, but he fore-
stalled me by running to the Venus and shoving
it on her fourth finger.   He then resumed his
post at the head of the Illois.

He was pale, but calm and resolute.   From
that moment he did not miss a single ball, and
the Spaniards were completely beaten.   The enthusiasm of the spectators was a fine sight; some
threw their caps in the air and shouted for joy,
while others wrung M. Alphonse's hands, calling
him the honor of the country.   If he had re-
pulsed an invasion I doubt if he would have
received warmer or sincerer congratulations.
The vexation of the vanquished added to the
splendor of the victory.

"We will play other games, my good fellow,"
he said to the Aragonese in a tone of superiority,
"but I will give you points."

I should have wished M. Alphonse to be more
modest, and I was almost pained by his rival's
humiliation.

The Spanish giant felt the insult deeply.   I

saw him pale beneath his tan. He looked sullenly at his racquet and clinched his teeth, then in a smothered voice he muttered:

"*Me lo pagarás.*"

M. de Peyrehorade's voice interrupted his son's triumph. Astonished at not finding him presiding over the preparation of the new carriage, my host was even more surprised on seeing him racquet in hand and bathed in perspiration. M. Alphonse hurried to the house, washed his hands and face, put on again his new coat and patent-leather shoes, and in five minutes we were galloping on the road to Puygarrig. All the racquet players of the town and a crowd of spectators followed us with shouts of joy. The strong horses which drew us could hardly keep ahead of the intrepid Catalans.

We were at Puygarrig, and the procession was about to set out for the town-hall, when M. Alphonse, striking his forehead, whispered to me:

"What a mess! I have forgotten the ring! It is on the finger of the Venus; may the devil carry her off! Do not tell my mother at any rate. Perhaps she will not notice it."

"You can send some one for it," I replied.

"My servant remained at Ille. I do not trust these here. Twelve hundred francs' worth of diamonds might well tempt almost any one. Moreover, what would they think of my forget-

fulness? They would laugh at me. They would
call me the husband of the statue. If it only is
not stolen! Fortunately, the rascals are afraid
of the idol. They do not dare approach it by an
arm's length. After all, it does not matter; I
have another ring."

The two ceremonies, civil and religious, were
accomplished with suitable pomp, and Mademoiselle de Puygarrig received the ring of a
Parisian milliner without suspecting that her
betrothed was making her the sacrifice of a love-
token. Then we seated ourselves at table, where
we ate, drank, and even sang, all at great length.
I suffered for the bride at the coarse merriment
which exploded around her; still, she faced it
better than I would have expected, and her embarrassment was neither awkward nor affected.

Perhaps courage comes with difficult situa-
tions.

The breakfast ended when heaven pleased.
It was four o'clock. The men went to walk in
the park, which was magnificent, or watched the
peasants, in their holiday attire, dance on the
lawn of the château. In this way we passed
several hours. Meanwhile the women were
eagerly attentive to the bride, who showed them
her presents. Then she changed her dress, and
I noticed that she had covered her beautiful hair
with a befeathered bonnet; for women are in no
greater hurry than to assume, as soon as pos-

sible, the attire which custom forbids their wearing while they are still young girls.

It was nearly eight o'clock when preparations were made to start for Ille. But first a pathetic· scene took place. Mlle. de Puygarrig's aunt, a very old and pious woman, who stood to her in a mother's place, was not to go with us. Before the departure she gave her niece a touching sermon on her wifely duties, from which sermon resulted a flood of tears and endless embraces.

M. de Peyrehorade compared this separation to the Rape of the Sabines.

At last, however, we got off, and, on the way, every one exerted himself to amuse the bride and make her laugh; but all in vain.

At Ille supper awaited us, and what a supper! If the coarse jokes of the morning had shocked me, I was now much more so by the equivocations and pleasantries of which the bride and groom were the principal objects. The bridegroom, who had disappeared for a moment before seating himself at the table, was pale, cold, and grave.

He drank incessantly some old Collioure wine almost as strong as brandy. I sat next to him, and thought myself obliged to warn him. "Be careful! they say that wine"—I hardly know what stupid nonsense I said to be in harmony with the other guests.

He touched my knee, and whispered:

"When we have left the table . . . let me have two words with you."

His solemn tone surprised me. I looked more closely at him, and noticed a strange alteration in his features.

"Do you feel ill?" I asked.

"No."

And he began to drink again.

Meanwhile, amidst much shouting and clapping of hands, a child of twelve, who had slipped under the table, held up to the company a pretty pink and white ribbon which he had untied from the bride's ankle. It was called her garter, and at once cut into pieces and distributed among the young men, who, following an old custom still preserved in some patriarchal families, ornamented their buttonholes with it. This was the time for the bride to flush up to the whites of her eyes. But her confusion was at its height when M. de Peyrehorade, having called for silence, sang several verses in Catalan, which he said were impromptu. Here is the meaning, if I understood it correctly :

"What is this, my friends? has the wine I have drunk made me see double? There are two Venuses here . . ."

The bridegroom turned his head suddenly with a frightened look, which made every one laugh.

"Yes," continued M. de Peyrehorade, "there are two Venuses under my roof. The one I found in the ground like a truffle ; the other, descended from heaven, has just divided among us her belt."

He meant her garter.

" My son, choose between the Roman Venus and the Catalan the one you prefer. The rascal takes the Catalan, and his choice is the best. The Roman is black, the Catalan is white. The Roman is cold, the Catalan enflames all who approach her."

This equivocal allusion excited such a shout, such noisy applause, and sonorous laughter, that I thought the ceiling would fall on our heads. Around the table there were but three serious faces, those of the newly-married couple and mine. I had a terrible headache ; and besides, I do not know why, a wedding always saddens me. This one, moreover, even disgusted me a little.

The final verses having been sung,—and very lively they were, I must say,—every one adjourned to the drawing-room to enjoy the withdrawal of the bride, who, as it was nearly midnight, was soon to be conducted to her room.

M. Alphonse drew me into the embrasure of a window, and, turning away his eyes, said :

" You will laugh at me— But I don't know what is the matter with me . . . I am bewitched ! "

My first thought was that he fancied himself threatened with one of those misfortunes of which Montaigne and Madame de Sévigné speak.

"All the world of love is full of tragic histories," etc.

"I thought only clever people were subject to this sort of accident," I said to myself.

To him I said: "You drank too much Collioure wine, my dear Monsieur Alphonse; I warned you against it."

"Yes, perhaps. But something much more terrible than that has happened."

His voice was broken. I thought him completely inebriated.

"You know about my ring?" he continued, after a pause.

"Well, has it been stolen?"

"No."

"Then you have it?"

"No—I—I cannot get it off the finger of that infernal Venus."

"You did not pull hard enough."

"Yes, indeed I did— But the Venus—she has bent her finger."

He stared at me wildly, and leaned against the window-sash to prevent himself from falling.

"What nonsense!" I said. "You pushed the ring on too far. You can get it off to-morrow with pincers. But be careful not to damage the statue."

"No, I tell you. The Venus's finger is crooked,

bent under; she clinches her hand, do you hear
me? . . . She is my wife apparently, since I have
given her my ring. . . . She will not return it."

I shivered, and, for a moment, I was all goose-
flesh. Then a great sigh from him brought me a
whiff of wine, and all my emotion disappeared.

The wretch, I thought, is dead drunk.

" You are an antiquarian, sir," added the bridegroom, in a mournful tone; " you understand
those statues; there is, perhaps, some hidden
spring, some deviltry which I do not know about.
Will you go and see?"

"Certainly," I replied. "Come with me."

" No, I would prefer to have you go alone."

I left the drawing-room.

The weather had changed during supper, and
a heavy rain had begun to fall. I was about to
ask for an umbrella, when a sudden thought
stopped me. I should be a great fool, I re-
flected, to go and verify what had been told me
by a drunken man! Besides, he may have wished
to play some silly trick on me to give cause for
laughter to the honest country people; and the
least that can happen to me from it is to be
drenched to the bone and catch a bad cold.

From the door I cast a glance at the statue
running with water, and I went up to my room
without returning to the drawing-room. I went
to bed; but sleep was long in coming. All the
scenes of the day passed through my mind. I

thought of the young girl, so pure and lovely, abandoned to a drunken brute. What an odious thing a marriage of convenience is! A mayor dons a tri-colored scarf, a priest a stole, and then the most virtuous girl in the world is delivered over to the Minotaur! What can two people who do not love each other find to say at a moment, which two lovers would buy at the price of their lives? Can a woman ever love a man whom she has once seen coarse? First impressions are never effaced, and I am sure M. Alphonse will deserve to be hated.

During my monologue, which I abridge very much, I had heard a great deal of coming and going in the house. Doors opened and shut, and carriages drove away. Then I seemed to hear on the stairs the light steps of a number of wo- men going towards the end of the hall opposite my room. It was probably the bride's train of attendants leading her to bed. After that they went downstairs again. Madame de Peyreho- rade's door closed. How troubled and ill at ease that poor girl must be, I thought. I tossed about in my bed with bad temper. A bachelor plays a stupid part in a house where a marriage is accomplished.

Silence had reigned for some time when it was disturbed by a heavy tread mounting the stairs. The wooden steps creaked loudly.

" What a clown ! " I cried to myself. " I

wager that he will fall on the stairs." All was
quiet again. I took up a book to change the
current of my thoughts. It was the county sta-
tistics, supplemented with an address by M. de
Peyrehorade on the Druidical remains of the
district of Prades. I grew drowsy at the third
page. I slept badly, and awoke repeatedly. It
might have been five o'clock in the morning, and
I had been awake more than twenty minutes,
when the cock crew. Day was about to dawn.
Then I heard distinctly the same heavy footsteps,
the same creaking of the stairs which I had heard
before I fell asleep. I thought it strange. Yawn-
ing, I tried to guess why M. Alphonse got up so
early. I could imagine no likely reason. I was
about to close my eyes again when my attention
was freshly excited by a singular trampling of
feet, which was soon intermingled with the ring-
ing of bells and the sound of doors opened
noisily; then I distinguished confused cries.

"My drunkard has set something on fire," I
thought, jumping out of bed. I dressed quickly
and went into the hall. From the opposite end
came cries and lamentations, and a heartrending
voice dominated all the others: "My son! my
son!" It was evident that an accident had
happened to M. Alphonse. I ran to the bridal
apartment: it was full of people. The first sight
which struck my gaze was the young man partly
dressed and stretched across the bed, the wood-

work of which was broken. He was livid and motionless. His mother sobbed and wept beside him. M. de Peyrehorade moved about frantically; he rubbed his son's temples with cologne water, or held salts to his nose. Alas! his son had long been dead. On a sofa at the other side of the room lay the bride, a prey to dreadful convulsions. She was making inarticulate cries, and two robust maid-servants had all the trouble in the world to hold her down. " Good heavens ! " I exclaimed, " what has happened ? "

I approached the bed and raised the body of the unfortunate young man : it was already stiff and cold. His clinched teeth and black face expressed the most fearful anguish. It was evident enough that his death had been violent and his agony terrible.

Nevertheless, no sign of blood was on his clothes. I opened his shirt, and on his chest I found a livid mark which extended around the ribs to the back. One would have said he had been squeezed in an iron ring. My foot touched something hard on the carpet; I stooped and saw it was the diamond ring. I dragged M. de Peyrehorade and his wife into their room, and had the bride carried there.

" You still have a daughter," I said to them. " You owe her your care." Then I left them alone.

To me it did not seem to admit of a doubt

that M. Alphonse had been the victim of a
murder whose authors had discovered a way to
introduce themselves into the bride's room during
the night. The bruises on the chest and their
circular direction, however, perplexed me, for
they could not have been made either by a club,
or an iron bar. Suddenly I remembered having
heard that at Valencia *bravi* used long leather
bags filled with sand to stun people whom they
had been paid to kill. Immediately I thought of
the Aragonese muleteer and his threat. Yet I
hardly dared suppose he would have taken such
a terrible revenge for a trifling jest.

I went through the house seeking everywhere
for traces of housebreaking, but could find none.
I descended to the garden to see if the assassins
could have made their entrance from there; but
there were no conclusive signs of it. In any
case, the evening's rain had so softened the
ground that it could not have retained any very
clear impress. Nevertheless, I noticed some
deeply marked footprints; they ran in two contrary directions, but on the same path. They
started from the corner of the hedge next the
racquet-court and ended at the door of the house.
They might have been made by M. Alphonse
when he went to get his ring from the finger of
the statue. Then again, the hedge at this spot
was narrower than elsewhere, and it must have
been here that the murderers got over it. Pass-

ing and repassing before the statue, I stopped
a moment to consider it. This time, I must confess, I could not contemplate its expression of
vicious irony without fear; and my mind being
filled with the horrible scene I had just witnessed,
I seemed to see in it a demoniacal goddess ap-
plauding the sorrow fallen on the house.

I returned to my room and stayed there till
noon. Then I left it to ask news of my hosts.
They were a little calmer. Mlle. de Puygarrig,
or I should say the widow of M. Alphonse, had
regained consciousness. She had even spoken
to the *procureur du roi* from Perpignan, then in
circuit at Ille, and this magistrate had received
her deposition. He asked for mine. I told him
what I knew, and did not hide from him my sus-
picions about the Aragonese muleteer. He ordered him to be arrested on the spot.

" Have you learned anything from Mme.
Alphonse ? " I asked the *procureur du roi*, when
my deposition was written and signed.

" 'That unfortunate young woman has gone
crazy," he said, smiling sadly. " Crazy, quite
crazy. This is what she says :

" She had been in bed for several minutes with
the curtains drawn, when the door of her room
opened and some one entered. Mme. Alphonse
was on the inside of the bed with her face turned
to the wall. Assured that it was her husband
she did not move. Presently the bed creaked as

if laden with a tremendous weight. She was terribly frightened, but dared not turn her head. Five minutes, or ten minutes perhaps—she has no idea of the time—passed in this way. Then she made an involuntary movement, or else it was the other person who made one, and she felt the contact of something as cold as ice : that is her expression. She buried herself against the wall trembling in all her limbs.

"Shortly afterwards, the door opened a second time, and some one came in who said, 'Good-evening, my little wife.' Then the curtains were drawn back. She heard a stifled cry. The person who was in the bed beside her sat up apparently with extended arms. Then she turned her head and saw her husband, kneeling by the bed with his head on a level with the pillow, held close in the arms of a sort of greenish-colored giant. She says, and she repeated it to me twenty times, poor woman !—she says that she recognized—do you guess whom ?—the bronze Venus, M. de Peyrehorade's statue. Since it has been here every one dreams about it. But to continue the poor lunatic's story. At this sight she lost consciousness, and probably she had already lost her mind. She cannot tell how long she remained in this condition. Returned to her senses she saw the phantom, or the statue as she insists on calling it, lying immovable, the legs and lower parts of the body on the bed, the bust and arms extended forward, and between the arms her husband, quite motionless. A cock crew. Then the statue left the bed, let fall the body, and went out. Mme. Alphonse rushed to the bell, and you know the rest."

The Spaniard was brought in ; he was calm, and defended himself with much coolness and presence of mind. He did not deny the remark which I had overheard, but he explained it, pretending that he did not mean anything except that the next day, when rested, he would beat his victor at a game of racquets. I remember that he added :

" An Aragonese when insulted does not wait till the next day to revenge himself. If I had believed that M. Alphonse wished to insult me I would have ripped him up with my knife on the spot."

His shoes were compared with the footprints in the garden ; the shoes were much the larger.

Finally, the innkeeper with whom the man lodged asserted that he had spent the entire night rubbing and dosing one of his mules which was sick. And, moreover, the Aragonese was a man of good reputation, well known in the neighborhood, where he came every year on business.

So he was released with many apologies.

I have forgotten to mention the statement of a servant who was the last person to see M. Alphonse alive. It was just as he was about to

join his wife, and calling to this man he asked
him in an anxious way if he knew where I was.
The servant answered that he had not seen me.
M. Alphonse sighed, and stood a minute without
speaking, then he said: "Well! the devil must
have carried him off also!"

I asked the man if M. Alphonse had on his
diamond ring. The servant hesitated; at last
he said he thought not; but for that matter he
had not noticed.

"If the ring had been on M. Alphonse's
finger," he added, recovering himself, "I should
probably have noticed it, for I thought he had
given it to Mme. Alphonse."

When questioning the man I felt a little of the
superstitious terror which Mme. Alphonse's statement had spread through the house. The *procureur du roi* smiled at me, and I was careful not
to insist further.

A few hours after the funeral of M. Alphonse
I prepared to leave Ille. M. de Peyrehorade's
carriage was to take me to Perpignan. Notwithstanding his feeble condition, the poor old man
wished to accompany me as far as the garden
gate. We crossed the garden in silence, he
creeping along supported by my arm. As we
were about to part I threw a last glance at the
Venus. I foresaw that my host, though he did
not share the fear and hatred which it inspired
in his family, would wish to rid himself of an ob-

13

ject which must ceaselessly recall to him a dreadful misfortune. My intention was to induce him to place it in a museum. As I hesitated to open the subject, M. de Peyrehorade turned his head mechanically in the direction he saw I was looking so fixedly. He perceived the statue, and immediately melted into tears. I embraced him, and got into the carriage without daring to say a word.

Since my departure I have not learned that any new light has been thrown on this mysterious catastrophe.

M. de Peyrehorade died several months after his son. In his will he left me his manuscripts, which I may publish some day. I did not find among them the article relative to the inscriptions on the Venus.

P. S.—My friend M. de P. has just written to me from Perpignan that the statue no longer exists. After her husband's death Madame de Peyrehorade's first care was to have it cast into a bell, and in this new shape it does duty in the church at Ille. "But," adds M. de P., "it seems as if bad luck pursues those who own the bronze. Since the bell rings at Ille the vines have twice been frozen."